Redemption

By

Elaine Pierson

Lacey Hannigan Novels
Growl
Change
Redemption

Other books by Elaine Pierson
Summer's Curse

This book is a work of fiction. Any references to real events, people or places are used fictitiously. Other names, characters, places, and incidents are the products of the author's imagination. Any resemblance to actual events, locales, or persons, living or dead, is entirely coincidental.

Visit the author's website: elainepiersonbooks.com for information about upcoming books

CHAPTER ONE

Cole looked around the tiny, dilapidated room that had become his prison. The rotten walls of the cabin looked as if they were barely able to hold the roof up. The room was dark even though he was pretty sure it was daylight outside, but since his days and nights ran together, he wasn't sure anymore. If it wasn't for Jesse's daily visits to torture him with unwanted information, he wouldn't even know how long he'd been there. His last count had been nine days but it seemed like forever since the last time Jesse was there.

He looked at his hands chained to the metal-framed bed post above his head, and winced. There was no longer skin covering the flesh of his wrist. It had been rubbed raw from where he had pulled relentlessly against the chains. He was now so used to the pain that it didn't even bother him much anymore. He let his gaze fall to his broken body laid out on the tiny, twin sized mattress.

All of the superficial wounds he had sustained in his fall had healed. The cuts and bruises were no longer visible. And the gash across his abdomen was now nothing more than a nasty scar. But his legs weren't as lucky. Both of them had been broken when he fell over the cliff. Without being braced to ensure proper healing, the broken bone in his left leg didn't heal correctly. It reconnected at an odd angle leaving him with a crooked leg. His right leg wasn't as bad, but it too hadn't healed properly. The thought of walking with a limp crossed Cole's mind and caused a low growl to rise in his throat.

He heard the cabin door squeak open, alerting him to Jesse's arrival. His jaw clenched tightly to hold in the string of profanities he wanted to hurl at him for waiting so long to come back. He desperately needed the small amount of water that Jesse had been bringing to him whenever he visited. His throat was dry and his lips were cracked from lack of moisture.

Jesse never brought food – he wanted to keep Cole weak so that he couldn't shift into his wolf form - but he almost always brought water. Cole listened as footsteps echoed through the empty cabin, getting closer. The door to his room eased opened and Jesse stepped inside with a huge grin on his face.

"What the hell took you so long?" Cole growled.

Jesse lifted his dark brows. "Don't tell me that you missed having me around?" he said, sarcastically.

Cole jerked against the chains around his wrists and growled, "Hell no I didn't miss you, asshole. I need water."

Jesse smiled as he crossed the room and opened the bottle of water he had in his hand. "Bottoms up," he said and poured it into Cole's open mouth.

After choking on the first couple of swallows, Cole chugged the water down. When the bottle was empty, Jesse dropped it to the floor and sat down on the make-shift seat by the bed, which was nothing more than a five gallon bucket that he had turned upside down to sit on.

Bracing himself for what was about to come, Cole turned his head away with his eyes closed. He knew what was going to happen now. It was what he hated most about Jesse's visits, when he had to listen to him talk about Lacey. He normally tried not to think about her because it hurt too much. But whenever Jesse was there, he didn't have a choice but to think about her. And every time he did, his already broken heart shattered even more.

He hated hearing about how easily Lacey had accepted his so-called death. According to Jesse, she never even bothered to look for his body. In a way, he couldn't blame her for not trying to find him. After all, she did see him fall over a hundred feet into the deadly water that raged through the mountain. But he had hoped that she would at least look for him.

The memory of the last time he saw her popped into his mind like it did a million times a day. The agony and devastation on her face as she looked down at him with tears streaming down her cheeks caused a massive ache in the center of his chest. He knew that he broke her heart when he let go of her arm, maybe that was why she didn't look for him...because he had hurt her. At least that was what he told himself to get through each day.

Believing that she didn't bother to look for him because she was angry was better than believing the alternative...that she had already forgotten about him and moved on with Jesse. Cole knew that she still loved him. She had already admitted that she still had feelings for Jesse the night she agreed to become his mate. And knowing that made hearing the things Jesse told him hurt even more.

"So, are you ready for today's report, brother? It's a doozy and I don't think you're going to like it. But I'm sure as hell going to love telling it to you" Jesse said with a sadistic grin.

Cole remained silent. It never did any good to protest hearing how in love Jesse and Lacey were. The first couple of days after he woke up in his prison, he threw major fits whenever Jesse mentioned Lacey's name. He cussed, yanked on his chains and even threatened to decapitate Jesse. But none of it did any good. Jesse just laughed and kept on talking.

Cole didn't even bother to fight hearing what he had to say anymore. There was nothing he could do to stop Jesse from talking and he knew it. So instead of wasting what little strength and energy he had left in fighting a losing battle, he kept his face turned away and stared at the wall across the dark room and waited for his daily torture to begin.

"As you know Lacey and I have gotten *really* close lately" Jesse said. Cole's body tensed. The muscles in his arms flexed as he balled his hands into fists above his head. The chains dug into his flesh. The sound of his teeth grinding against each other could be heard in the silence of the cabin.

Jesse smiled and continued, "We've pretty much picked up right where we left off before you stole her from me and forced her to come here with you. Anyway, I want you to be the first to know that she has agreed to become my mate. In a week or so, we will be mated. And after that, I'll put an end to your suffering just like I promised."

Cole tried to keep the despair from his voice as he spoke, "why don't you just kill me now and get it over with?" He'd rather be dead than have to smell Lacey's scent mixed with Jesse's and know that he truly had lost her forever. Just the thought of it hurt so bad that he felt as if his chest was caving in on him.

Jesse smirked. "Oh no, you're not getting off the hook that easy. I'm enjoying myself way too much to kill you now. I had to go through weeks of hell knowing that the woman I loved was with you. Not knowing what you were doing with her drove me crazy day after day. Now it's your turn to know what that feels like. The only difference is you *will* know what I'm doing with her because I'm going to share every dirty detail with you. I want you to suffer knowing that Lacey will be sharing my bed very soon."

Cole couldn't take it anymore. An image of Lacey and Jesse in bed together flashed in his mind. He jerked against the chains that bound him to the bed. With his nostrils flared, he pierced Jesse with a hate-filled glare. The veins in his neck protruded as he yelled, "You son-of-a-bitch! Lay one finger on her and you're a dead man!" he threatened.

Jesse laughed, "Too late for that. I haven't been able to keep my hands off of her. I love the softness of her skin and the way she blushes when I brush my lips softly over hers."

Cole growled out loud, deep lines creased his forehead. Jesse laughed before standing up to leave. "I can see that I've shared enough of my love life with you for one day." He crossed the room and stopped by the bedroom door. "I might not be back for a day or so, you know how it is when you have a woman at home who needs you. It's hard to get away sometimes. But I'm sure you'll be fine on your own, won't you?"

"Just get the hell out!" Cole snarled.

Jesse walked out and slammed the door behind him. Once outside of the cabin, he made sure to lock the door before placing the veil of bushes and tree limbs back in front of the entrance. He stepped back from the cabin and surveyed his work.

The old hunters lodge was completely hidden from view with the decade's worth of wild bushes and weeds that grew up the sides and over the top. The extra foliage and tree limbs that Jesse had placed around it added to its camouflage. The cabin was basically invisible. It looked like a large mass of bushes, much like other areas of the mountain. No one would know a cabin was there even if they passed right by it. Jesse took one last look to make sure the door of the cabin was completely covered before leaving.

The smile that he'd worn while talking with Cole instantly vanished. His lips set into a hard line. He wished that what he'd told his brother was true, that Lacey and he were going to be mated. That she still loved him. But it was nothing more than a lie to break Cole's spirit and make him suffer. The truth was he was no closer to winning Lacey back now than he'd been when he first arrived on the mountain. And with each day that passed, he grew more frustrated…and desperate.

*****

Cole steamed with fury as he stared at the door where Jesse had been standing a few minutes earlier. His chest heaved with every labored breath he took. He had never hated his brother more than he did at that moment. The thought of Jesse kissing Lacey and holding her in his arms, ripped him apart inside. And it put him into a murderous state of mind. A feeling he hadn't felt in a long time, not since Lacey came into his life.

Different images of how he wanted to kill Jesse played out in his mind, but none of them seemed to satisfy the rage building inside him. They were just thoughts in his head, not reality. The reality of the situation was that he was trapped and Jesse was free to do whatever he wanted. Cole let out a guttural growl and pulled as hard as he could against the chains on his wrists, but just like the hundreds of other times he'd done so, nothing happened.

He let his head fall back to the mattress, feeling defeated. The chains used to secure him were the same kind that he had used to keep his newbie werewolves in line. They were unbreakable, even for him. He let out a deep breath and closed his eyes, and as soon as he did, Lacey's face popped into his mind. Her long blond hair shimmered in the sunlight as her blue eyes stared at him. She smiled and Cole's chest grew tight. "Oh, Lacey" he whispered to himself.

The sound of his own voice brought him out of his daydream. He opened his eyes, lifted his upper lip into a snarl and shook his head from side to side. "I won't let Jesse have you" he said, Lacey's face still fresh in his mind. "I'll never let that happen."

Since the day he woke up chained to the bed and realized that he couldn't get free, he had pretty much accepted the fact that he was going to die, and that Jesse had won. And up until now, there was nothing he could do about it. In the beginning, his wounds had prevented him from attempting any kind of escape. But that wasn't the case anymore. Most of his wounds had healed and now that the threat of actually losing Lacey forever seemed like a real possibility, he was more determined than ever to find a way to escape and get back to her. To fight for her.

He glanced up at the chains around his wrists once more before dropping his eyes to his lower body. There was nothing he could do about the chains, but his legs were a different story. Knowing that both his legs had been broken, Jesse didn't bother to secure them. But even though they were free, Cole hadn't tried to move them at all. The fear of seeing his legs move in an unnatural way or worst, not moving at all, had prevented him from testing his ability to use them. But now he realized that his legs were his only hope of ever getting out of there.

Cole clenched his jaw tightly and ground his teeth together as he stared at his legs and forced all the strength he had into trying to move them. They felt heavy and weird, like they didn't belong on his body. Inch by slow agonizing inch, he shakily lifted them from the mattress.

Sweat poured down the side of his face from the strain of holding his legs up. It killed him to know that something as simple as lifting his own legs was taking so much out of him. He was so weak from lack of food that it took all the strength he had to hold them in the air for just a few seconds.

Unable to hold them up any longer, he let his legs fall back to the mattress with an exhausted breath. After taking a few deep breaths, he lifted them again…and again. The pain that ripped through him as he bent his legs at the knees was excruciating, but he didn't stop. He continued to work his legs out as he pushed past the pain with only one thought in mind…Lacey. There was nothing he wouldn't do for her, and no pain he wouldn't endure.

He still didn't know how he was going to escape, but he was going to be ready for when the opportunity presented itself. The muscles in his legs began to burn as he forced them to move faster in a cycling motion as if he were riding a bike. The bones in his knees protested the movement, making a popping sound every time he bent his legs. His heart raced as adrenaline pumped throughout his body, urging him on.

After nearly half an hour of vigorous exercise, he let his legs fall to the bed. A small grin spread across his face at his tiny accomplishment. "I'm coming, Lacey" he said to himself with a tired, ragged breath. "One way or another I'll get free and find my way back to you."

CHAPTER TWO

Lacey sat on the bed in her cabin wondering how in the world she was going to make it through another day of searching for Cole when she knew the probability of actually finding him wasn't good. It had been almost a week and a half since he fell off a cliff during a fight with his twin brother, Jesse. She had tried to save them both, but after fighting her own battle with Sasha – a female wolf hell bent on killing her - and then using her telekinetic powers to stop her friends from the mountain pack and the Carol Springs pack from killing each other, she didn't have the strength to pull them up.

Lacey closed her eyes as Cole's last words went through her mind for the hundred time. *I love you. Always remember that.* He'd spoken those words to her seconds before he pried her fingers from his wrist and fell to the roaring waters below. She forced her eyes open. She didn't want the image of him falling to replay in her mind again. Every time it did, she lost another piece of her heart…and perhaps some of her sanity.

The last week had been hard on her, both physically and emotionally. And it was only because of her determination not to have any more deaths on her conscious that she had managed to keep a tight hold on her powers. From time to time she felt that hold slipping. When she did, she forced herself to see the faces of all the people who had died because of her – Sasha, Fiona, Carly, and Tia – and that renewed her will to resist her powers.

Everyone on the mountain was already cautious around her.

Trevor and the cousins; Devon and Tyron had returned to Carol Springs. They didn't say anything but Lacey had the feeling they didn't like her anymore. They made it clear that they didn't agree with her decision to stay on the mountain. Trevor just used the fact that Tonya was pregnant and in need of his attention as an excuse to leave. Lacey was hurt over the loss of their friendships but she didn't have time to dwell on it. They made the decision to leave and she had to accept it. Besides, all of her time was spent searching for Cole. That alone, kept her busy and prevented her from thinking too much about losing her friends.

She tried to settle into the position of alpha female of the Black Hills pack, but without Cole by her side she had no real interest in leading the pack. But at the same time, she didn't want to give up the position. She still had hope that Cole was alive and that she would find him. But as the days passed by and everyone else got back to their normal lives, she was beginning to lose some of that hope. Almost everyone had given up on helping her search for Cole. Everyone except Maggie, Luke, and Jeremiah.

They were her support team. Even though neither one of them really believed they would find him, they helped her anyway. And she loved them for it. She just wished that Jeremiah and Luke would stop looking at her like they thought she was going to lose it at any minute and kill them all. She had more control over her powers than they gave her credit for, but she didn't tell them that.

Maggie pretty much stayed by her side all the time. Worry and concern was permanently etched on her face every time she looked at Lacey. But she wasn't afraid of her powers, she was afraid of what was happening to Lacey's mental state of mind. She had already been witness to the nightmares that kept her awake at night. Lacey had awoken several times in the last week, screaming Cole's name. Each time Maggie heard the agony in her voice, it made her chest ache. She hated to see her friend hurting so badly.

Jesse, on the other hand didn't seem to have the same sensitivity to Lacey's anguish as Maggie. Sure, he helped in the search every day and even held Lacey a few times when she cried, but Maggie could tell that he didn't really care if they found Cole or not. And so could Lacey. She knew he was only helping for her sake. Sometimes, knowing that made her mad.

She didn't understand how Jesse could be so unbothered by what happened to his brother. Even if they did fight a lot and claimed to hate each other, she still felt like he should feel something. After all, they were family. But all she ever saw on his face was a smile, and that disturbed her. However, what really bothered her was the uneasy feeling she was starting to get whenever she was around him.

When she was human the only way she could tell Jesse and Cole apart – since they're identical twins - was the scar that crossed Jesse's throat. But now as a werewolf she could tell them apart because of their scents. Each person's scent is unique, and while Jesse's and Cole's scents are similar, they are not the same. And knowing that piece of information has left Lacey feeling a little confused. The last few times she was near Jesse, she could swear she smelled Cole's scent on him. She asked him about it several times.

And each time, Jesse played off her concerns by saying that since his and Cole's scents were so similar and Lacey hadn't been around them both at the same time long enough to detect the differences, she was confusing them in her mind. His explanation seemed plausible but it still bothered her. Something didn't seem right. She just couldn't put her finger on it.

It was strange how much her feelings for Jesse had changed since the night on the cliff. Up till that night, she was convinced that she was still in love with him. Not as in love as she was with

Cole, but Jesse had owned a piece of her heart. Now she didn't know how she felt about him.

She wasn't in love with him anymore, she was sure of that. Her every thought from the time she woke up every morning until she went to sleep at night was of Cole. He was the one she was in love with, the one she wanted to be with. It took losing him for her to finally realize that he had been the one she wanted all along. The *only* one she wanted.

Every time she thought about Jesse, she was hit with a wave of conflicting emotions. She still cared about him but knowing what she knew about him and his past made her question whether or not she wanted him in her life anymore. She had already made it clear to him that all she could offer him was friendship.

However, she wasn't even sure if she could offer him that. That night on the cliff, she saw a side to him she didn't know existed. It was a side of him that scared her. He wasn't the same man she met in Carol Springs. He was different now.

The memory of Jesse screaming at her to drop Cole burned in her mind all the time, making her question just how much she really knew about him. She often found herself wanting to lash out at him for his cruel outburst when he was hanging over the cliff, which is why she had spent most of the last week and a half avoiding him as much as possible.

Lacey ran her hands down her face roughly and let out a deep breath as she scooted to the edge of the bed. It was time to face another day whether she was ready for it or not. She stood up and looked across the room at Kindal, still asleep on the roll-away cot.

Kindal had been her roommate for the last week even though Lacey insisted that she wanted to be left alone. But after Jesse made a big deal about wanting to stay with her in the cabin 'to keep her safe' so he said, and was about to cause a major fight with Jeremiah and Luke when they said no, Lacey had agreed to let Kindal stay with her instead.

She didn't need either one of them to keep her safe, but to avoid more trouble she took on a roommate. She hated that they were still treating her like a weak human.

"You're up already?" Kindal asked as she wiped the sleep from her eyes and looked out the window to see that it was still dark outside.

Lacey met her eyes briefly then continued to make up her bed, "why should that surprise you? I've been up before the sun every day since…" she let her words die off without completing her sentence.

Kindal's face softened. "I know, it's just…I thought since you still haven't found him that maybe you would give up soon. You know, move on with her life."

Lacey's head snapped up. "What! I'm never going to give up. Not until I find Cole. Dead or alive. Why is it so hard for everyone to understand that?" Her voice was sharper than she intended.

Kindal got out of bed and approached her. "We're worried about you, okay. You're not letting yourself get more than two or three hours of sleep a night. You spend all day running around the mountain searching for something you might never find."

"Something?" Lacey asked, with narrowed eyes, "Cole isn't a thing, he's a person. And I *will* find him." She shook her head from side to side and brushed past Kindal on her way to the kitchen. She stopped at the table and turned around, her anger quickly rising, "You know, since the day I found out about werewolves, I thought that Cole was the only one that truly was an animal because of the things he'd done, but that's not true…you and everyone else around here are just as much an animal as Cole ever was. Your willingness to leave him out there, to abandon him when he needs help, proves how much of an animal you all are."

Before Kindal could respond, Lacey stormed into the bathroom and slammed the door. Kindal sat back down on the cot and rested her head in her hands. She didn't know what to say around Lacey any more. Everything she said seemed to set her off. She was beginning to think that the Lacey she once knew was gone. Kindal's hatred for Cole grew even more with the thought. She blamed him for the changes in Lacey. If he hadn't kidnapped her, she wouldn't be the hard, distant person she was now.

When Kindal first moved in with Lacey, she had asked her how she could love someone who had hunted down and killed innocent humans. The reminder of how they met made Lacey cringe. She had shaken her head sadly and tried to explain to Kindal that Cole had changed. That he wasn't the same man anymore. And that he had given her his word he would never hunt humans again.

Kindal still didn't understand and Lacey couldn't tell her why Cole had started hunting humans in the first place. She couldn't bring herself to talk about the day he told her that Jesse had paid human hunters to kill their father. She still hadn't confronted Jesse with the accusation yet and didn't feel comfortable talking about it until she spoke with him first.

Besides, she didn't really think Kindal would believe her anyway. So she ended the conversation by saying that who she loved was her business. She didn't like being snappy with Kindal but she also didn't like having to defend herself for loving Cole.

Kindal was lost in thought when the bathroom door opened and Lacey stepped into the room. She glanced in Kindal's direction before reaching for the door of the cabin. She couldn't stay in the room with her old friend any longer. She couldn't risk the chance she might lose control of herself if they got into another argument.

"Lacey" Kindal said softly, "I'm sorry. I didn't mean to upset you."

Lacey kept her back to her. She looked down at her shaky hand on the doorknob. She was trying extra hard to force her powers back. She didn't want to be mad at Kindal, she was her friend. Someone she cared about. But she couldn't stand hearing her or anyone else talk about Cole like he was nothing. It made her angry and her anger triggered her powers. She did have more control over them now, but she had to work hard to keep it.

When Lacey didn't respond, Kindal continued, "You know I would never do or say anything to hurt you on purpose. I really am sorry."

Lacey glanced over her shoulder. The sadness on Kindal's face touched a nerve deep inside her. She eased her grip on the doorknob and turned around. The edgy feeling inside her was forced to the back of her mind. "I know you're not a bad person, Kindal. But neither is Cole. Maybe he used to be, but he's not anymore. I love him. And I know how much you hate hearing me say that but it's true. I'm not asking you to like him, hell I'm not even asking you to help look for him. I'm just asking that you not say anything negative about him around me. You're one of my best friends and I love you, but I won't tolerate you or anyone else talking bad about him."

Kindal nodded and eased her arms around Lacey's neck. "I won't say another word, I promise."

Lacey hugged her back before heading into the kitchen to fix breakfast. She opened cabinet after cabinet to find them all bare. She then went to the tiny fridge in the corner and again found nothing. She hadn't been to the village in days to buy groceries and apparently Kindal hadn't bought anything either. She leaned against the sink with her arms crossed over her chest and sighed.

"We can go hunting" Kindal suggested.

The memory of her hunt with Cole flashed in Lacey's mind - the dead rabbit, the taste of coppery blood in her mouth, the way she freaked out afterwards. She quickly shook her head. "No, I've tried that. It's not for me" she said with certainty.

Kindal let out a small laugh. "What do you mean it's not for you? You're a wolf and wolves hunt. It's what we do, especially when there isn't any human food to eat."

Lacey gave her a hard look. "Like I said, I tried it and I didn't like it."

"What didn't you like about it? Having to eat the meat raw or having to chase it down? I know I hate it when I'm after something that's faster than me" Kindal babbled.

"Killing" Lacey said in a thick voice, "I hate the killing part."

"Oh" Kindal said in a low voice, "I guess I can understand how you might not be used to it yet. But it does get easier over time."

"Why does everyone keep saying that?" Lacey said with an edge to her raised voice. "Killing is not easy, whether it's an animal for lunch or a person you're in a fight with, killing is *never* easy."

Kindal could sense the power rising up in Lacey. It was strange how she could feel the power radiating from her body, but it was a constant reminder of how strong Lacey's powers really were…and how dangerous she was. Kindal knew she had to calm her down before things got out of control. A change of subject was definitely needed. "Have you talked to Jesse lately?"

Lacey pushed away from the sink and grabbed her shoes from the floor. "I talk to him at least once every day. Why?"

Kindal looked uncomfortable as she spoke. "I meant have you talked to him about anything other than the search for Cole." She paused and waited for Lacey to respond, but she didn't say anything. Instead, she kept her head low with her hair blocking her face as she put her shoes on.

Kindal had the feeling she was trying to avoid the question. "Lacey...I know we've already had this talk but he really misses you. And since both of you are my friends, I feel caught in the middle. I want you both to be happy." She sighed sadly, "You don't know what he went through after you left. It really tore him up. And finding you here with Cole hasn't made him feel any better. He loves you. And from what I remember from your time at the warehouse, you love him too."

Lacey stood tall and narrowed her eyes at Kindal. "Are you trying to play matchmaker now?" She didn't wait for Kindal to answer. "Because if you are, you can stop it. What happened between Jesse and me in Carol Springs is in the past. It feels like a lifetime ago. I've changed so much since then. I feel like I've aged years just within the last few months." She sighed, "I guess learning bad things about the people you love will do that to a person."

The last remark caught Kindal's attention. "What do you mean by that? What exactly have you learned? And who are you referring to?"

Lacey stared at her briefly then looked away. She didn't want to go into detail about everything she'd learned about Jesse. Not when she had more important things to do...like picking up her search for Cole where she left off yesterday. "Nothing, just drop it."

Kindal opened her mouth to respond then closed it when the door of the cabin opened and Maggie walked in. She smiled at Lacey before sparing a dismissive glance in Kindal's direction.

The two of them were far from being friends. Maggie didn't trust Kindal. And Kindal didn't like Maggie because she felt as if she had taken her place as Lacey's best friend.

"Good morning, ladies" Maggie said as she placed a large plate on the kitchen table. She grinned at Lacey and removed the aluminum foil that covered the plate. "I noticed your fridge was empty last night and figured you might need breakfast this morning."

Lacey returned her smile and sat down at the table. "You're a lifesaver, Maggie." She looked at the stack of BLT sandwiches in front of her as her mouth watered with anticipation.

Kindal rolled her eyes and started toward the door.

"Where are you going?" Lacey asked through a mouthful of sandwich.

Kindal looked over her shoulder at her. "Outside. I think I'll catch my own breakfast." She narrowed her eyes at Maggie then returned her gaze to Lacey, "I'm in the mood to kill something."

Lacey shrugged her shoulders and took another bite of her sandwich. "Suite yourself, that means more for me."

Kindal walked out, letting the door slam shut behind her.

"I don't think she likes me very much" Maggie said with a satisfied smile as she sat down beside Lacey.

"Don't worry about Kindal. I think her attitude was meant for me. We didn't get off to a good start this morning."

"Anything that you want to talk about?" Maggie asked.

"Nope!" Lacey popped the last bite of sandwich into her mouth before grabbing another one.

"Alright then." Maggie reached into a brown leather bag that she had brought with her and pulled out a map. She spread it out on the table. "Luke and I were up most of the night going over this map of the mountain. We marked all the places that we've already searched so that we don't keep searching over the same areas." She pointed to an area circled in red, "I think we should check out this area today. I know it's a good ways from the river but no one has covered it yet."

Lacey was stunned silent as she stared at all the black x's on the map. Over ninety percent of it was covered with x's. Until that moment, she hadn't realized how much of the mountain she had already searched. "There isn't much left to search, is there?" she said in a low voice and ran her fingers over the few unmarked areas of the map.

"I'm afraid not" Maggie said as she took in the devastated look on Lacey's face.

Maggie started to fold the map up but Lacey stopped her. She pointed to an area on the map that had been separated from the areas they were searching by a broad black line. There were no red marks or black x's in that area. It hadn't been searched yet. "Why is this area of the mountain separated from the rest?"

Maggie looked uncomfortable when she noticed where Lacey had pointed. "That side of the mountain is off limits" she said and hoped that Lacey would let it go, but she knew that she wouldn't.

"Off limits? Why?" Lacey asked with curiosity. The fact that Maggie was trying to avoid eye contact with her peeked her interest even more.

Maggie was getting more uncomfortable with every passing second. She didn't want to be the one who had to tell Lacey why that section of the mountain was off limits. She was afraid it would upset her. "It just is, okay. We can't go there. It's not like Cole could have made it all the way over there anyway. Besides, we already have today's search area mapped out."

Lacey raised her brows, causing her forehead to wrinkle. She could tell that Maggie was keeping something from her.

"Maggie" she stretched her name out. "Why is it off limits?" she asked again.

Maggie lowered her head as she spoke, "because bad things happened there."

"What kind of bad things?" Lacey prompted.

Maggie raised her head slowly and frowned. "Cole"

Lacey tensed at hearing his name. "What the hell does he have to do with it?"

Maggie let out a deep sigh. "That side of the mountain used to be open to the public. The *human* public. Hunters would come here to hunt bears. Campers would bring their families here on vacation."

"That doesn't explain what Cole has to do with that area being off limits" Lacey said in an irritated tone.

Maggie's frown deepened. "It's where he went on his rampage after his father died. A lot of human hunters were killed. The deaths attracted more hunters to the area, but they weren't like the others. The new hunters had been hired to hunt down and kill the wolf responsible for killing the humans. There had been witnesses to one of Cole's attacks. " She paused as she remembered the sadness on her father's face when he told her the story.

"Many of our pack were killed in retaliation. For a long time after that, everyone was afraid to shift into their wolf form. The pack stayed away from that area and eventually the hunters left. But the damage to the pack had been done. No one felt safe. So the elders at that time forbade anyone to ever set foot on that side of the mountain and since then, no one has. And because of all the deaths and the fact that the hunters never caught the wolf they believed was responsible, the humans stopped coming here."

Lacey listened as the images of what Maggie described played out in her mind. Her chest tightened at the reminder of the chaos Cole had created. He had already told her about the killing spree he went on after losing his father, but he never mentioned the price the pack had to pay because of it. She hated hearing that some of his pack had been killed because of his actions. But now she understood why when they first arrived on the mountain, no one wanted them there.

"He was hurting, Maggie. Losing his father destroyed him. I don't agree with what he did back then, but I can understand his rage. Losing someone that you love is hard but having that person maliciously taken from you by someone that you trusted is even harder" Lacey said.

"What are talking about?" Maggie asked with a confused expression.

Lacey took a second to think about how much of what Cole had confided in her that she wanted to share with Maggie. It didn't take long for her to decide that she wanted to tell her everything. Cole had told her that no one but he and Jeremiah knew about Jesse's involvement in their father's death. But she didn't want to keep that information bottled up inside her anymore. She wanted to be able to talk to someone about it. And Maggie was a friend of Cole's and she knew she could trust her.

Lacey let out a deep breath and told Maggie everything. It was a long, tense conversation.

"I knew there was a reason I didn't like Jesse" Maggie said and shook her head angrily, her blond curls bounced around her face. "How could he do that to his own father?"

"I don't know…but I'm going to find out" Lacey said with certainty. She glanced to the window and saw sunlight peeping through the curtains, she shook her head. "Just not right now. I have other things to do at the moment." She stood up and grabbed the map. She studied it hard for a few minutes then dropped it back to the table. "Time to go." She glanced over at Maggie, "you and Luke can search the spot you circled in red on the map."

"What about you?" Maggie asked.

Lacey looked away as she committed the directions on the map to memory. "I have somewhere else in mind. I'll catch up with you later" she said and lifted her shirt over her head and tossed it to the floor. Within seconds she was completely naked.

In the last week she had learned to get over a lot of the little quirks she had with being a werewolf. No longer bothered by her own nudity, she gave Maggie a small smile before dropping to the floor and shifting into a beautiful white wolf. She ran out of the cabin and into the woods with her destination clear in mind. She didn't know what was drawing her to the forbidden part of the mountain, but she had to check it out.

CHAPTER THREE

Jesse broke through the tree line in front of Lacey's cabin and came to an abrupt stop when he saw Luke, Jeremiah and a couple others standing on the porch. "Damn it" he whispered to himself. He had been hoping to have a few moments alone with Lacey before the ruse of another search began.

He forced the growl that built in his throat away and put on the fake smile he was used to wearing around everyone. One of the things he had learned in the last week was that he needed to earn everyone's trust if he was going to win Lacey back. She had become very close with some of the members of his birth pack, his cousin Jeremiah's family, in particular. It occurred to him that if they liked him, maybe they could help convince her to move on with him.

Somewhere deep inside, Jesse knew that he was changing. He never would have imagined that falling in love could turn him into the man he was becoming. Deceitful and malicious. Losing Lacey had brought out a part of himself that he didn't even know existed. Before he met her, everything he did was to help others. He had spent twenty years doing good things. It had been his way of atoning for the sins of his past.

But now, none of the good he'd done mattered anymore. In his mind, it was all wiped away the moment he found Cole half dead at the bottom of the cliff and decided to keep him prisoner. That one decision made in a moment of extreme desperation changed everything he thought he knew about himself. When he really thought about it, he had to accept the fact that he wasn't much different from the brother he hated. He would do whatever he had to do to get what he wanted. And what he wanted was Lacey. Nothing was going to stand in his way.

Jesse made his way to the porch. "Jeremiah, Luke" He gave a nod to acknowledge them.

"You're still here?" Luke asked, sarcastically. "I figured since I hadn't seen you since early yesterday that you might have come to your senses and left. I mean, we all know that you're wasting your time here. Lacey is never going to leave with you."

Jesse pretended not to let the remark bother him, but inside it cut deep. He fought back the urge to smack the grin off Luke's face. "Yeah well, it's good to see you too, Luke." He turned his attention to Jeremiah, "Is Lacey inside?" he asked and started for the door.

"No, she's already left this morning."

"Where did she go?" Jesse asked, "And who is with her?" Jealousy seeped into him, making him anxious to hear the answer.

"I don't know" Jeremiah responded. "She was gone when we got here. Maggie said she left on her own." He met Jesse's eyes as he spoke his next words, "she doesn't need a baby-sitter. She is more than capable of taking care of herself."

"She shouldn't be roaming around this damn mountain by herself" Jesse said and started down the steps.

Jeremiah grabbed his arm to stop him. "Leave her alone. She needs time, don't you understand that?" He released his hold on Jesse's arm and ran his hand through his hair. "Look Jesse, I know that you love her. I know all about everything that happened in Carol Springs but you have to understand that she fell in love with Cole, and until she accepts the fact that he's gone, she's not going to give you the time of day." He sighed, "If you really want a chance at getting her back…then back off. Let her have the time she needs. And when she's ready, be here to comfort her. But if you try to smother her with attention that she doesn't want right now, you're only going to push her further away."

Jesse listened as Jeremiah spoke. He hated hearing what he said, but he did have a good point. He knew Lacey well enough to know that not playing by her rules meant he would get kicked out of the game early. And he was in it for the long haul. He nodded at his cousin, "you're right. Thanks for the advice." Jesse smiled, his plan was working. Jeremiah was on his side. Hopefully he could use that to his advantage.

"Dad, what the hell are you doing?" Luke grumbled and looked at Jeremiah. "Why are you helping him? Let him screw up so Lacey will make him leave."

Jesse narrowed his eyes at Luke a second before he jumped from the porch to join Kindal and Scotty, who were waiting for him at the edge of the woods. He couldn't risk anyone seeing the hatred on his face that he had for Luke.

Jeremiah looked at his son, "not now, Luke. We'll talk about it later."

Luke shook his head. "No, we won't...because if you think for one second that I approve of that bastard being with Lacey, you're crazy." He paused to glare across the yard at Jesse before he turned his attention back to his father. "Don't you feel any loyalty to Cole at all? He was your family. Hell, you even gave up your position as alpha to him."

"Jesse is my family too" Jeremiah responded. "And he loves Lacey. Why do you think he came all the way out here to find her? I'm just trying to do what's best for the pack. I care about Lacey, but she's unstable right now...and dangerous. Maybe Jesse can help her get through this hard time, make her happy again so that she's not so quick to lose her temper. Don't you understand that our survival depends on her controlling her powers?"

"Really? Is that all there is to it? Or are you hoping that he can get her to leave with him so you and mom can reclaim your positions?"

"That has nothing to do with it!" Jeremiah scolded.

"I sure as hell hope not because if Lacey leaves, I'll leave with her. And so will Maggie. I made a promise to Cole that I would take care of her if anything ever happened to him, and I intend to keep it" Luke said and turned away from his father.

Just then, Maggie opened the door of the cabin and stepped out with a tray of coffee mugs. Before she could offer Luke one, he took the tray from her and sat it down on the porch. He grabbed her hand, "let's go. We don't have time for coffee."

Maggie looked startled as he tugged her down the steps of the porch. She followed behind him as he stormed across the short distance to the trees. She had never seen Luke so upset before. A million questions entered her mind but from the look on Luke's face she knew now was not the time to ask any of them. She stayed silent and let him lead her into the woods while Jeremiah stared after them.

"What the hell was that all about?" Scotty asked and tilted his head toward the porch where Jeremiah was still standing.

"I don't know. Looked like a father/son thing to me" Jesse said with a shake of his head. "Maybe little Luke finally got put in his place." He hoped. He didn't want Luke causing any trouble for him.

Scotty laughed, "And *that* my friends, is why I don't want any kids. I cannot deal with the kind of attitude that kid has. What is his problem anyway?"

"Do you think maybe it has something to do with Lacey?" Kindal asked.

"No. I'm sure it has nothing to do with her" Jesse said quickly. "Why would you ask that anyway?"

Kindal kept her eyes low as she spoke. She could feel Jesse watching her, waiting on her to respond. "No reason. It's just that I've noticed Luke is very protective of her. And sometimes I get the feeling that Jeremiah doesn't really want her here. He's scared of her. Everyone here is."

"Hell, I would be lying if I said that I wasn't a little scared of Lacey too, especially when she's pissed" Scotty said with an uneasy chuckle. "But she's still our friend. And even though right now she acts like she doesn't want us here, I'm not going anywhere until I know that she's going to be okay."

Kindal felt uncomfortable as her gaze shifted between Jesse and Scotty. She had something to say and knew it was going to hurt Jesse and probably make him angry. He was so quick to lose his temper lately whenever Lacey was mentioned that she wasn't sure she wanted to speak.

Scotty noticed Kindal biting on her lip. He knew the only time she did that was when she was nervous. "What's up, Kindal? Something on your mind?" he asked.

Her eyes met his for a brief second before she turned her attention to Jesse. She let out a deep breath and said what she needed to say. "I think we all keep hoping that once Lacey finally accepts that Cole is dead, she will go back to the way she used to be, the way we remember her. And I'm just not sure that is ever going to happen. She's not the same person we knew in Carol Springs. She's been through things that have changed her. When we first met her, she was a weak, fragile teenage girl. Now she's an alpha female of an entire pack. She's strong-willed and feisty. And sometimes down-right stubborn. She has had to fight and even kill to survive. Things like that can change a person forever."

The muscles in Jesse's jaw clenched tightly as he narrowed his eyes at Kindal. "What exactly are you trying to say? That we should just forget about her and leave? And go about our lives as if we never met her?"

"I don't know" Kindal whispered. The thought of leaving and never seeing Lacey again made her want to cry. She missed the friendship they used to have. "I really don't know what we should do. I don't want to leave but I also don't know that our being here is going to change anything. Lacey has made it clear that she's not going back to Carol Springs with us. This is her home now, she wants to stay here."

"This is not her home!" Jesse yelled, making Kindal flinch at the harshness of his voice. "She *will* leave with us. She just needs more time, that's all. And if you don't want to wait for her then you can leave now, no one is stopping you."

Scotty put a restraining hand on Jesse's shoulder. "Hey buddy, calm down. Kindal is on your side and so am I. She's just saying what we already know. There is no reason to get mad at her."

Jesse turned his gaze to Scotty. He knew the goofy smile on his face was meant to diffuse the situation. Jesse let out a deep sigh and dropped his head, then took a breath to calm himself. "You're right." He turned to Kindal, "I'm sorry. I shouldn't have yelled at you like that."

She nodded in acceptance of his apology. "It's okay" she said and looked around to see that they were now alone. Jeremiah was nowhere in sight. "So what are we supposed to do now? Do you want us to try and track Lacey down or help Maggie and Luke wherever they're searching?"

Jesse was quiet for a minute, then he shook his head. "Neither. I want you two to mingle. Get to know some of the pack members here, make friends if possible. Jeremiah was right about one thing, Lacey needs to be left alone for a while. And as far as searching for Cole, we're done with that. He's dead and gone. And we're not wasting any more of our time looking for him. Eventually, Lacey will give up too."

Scotty looked at Jesse with raised brows, "you want us to make friends? Why?"

Jesse smiled at the confused look on his face. "Because I'm going to try a change in tactic with Lacey. Since we arrived here we have been following her every step, trying to convince her to leave with us. And it hasn't worked. Maybe the old saying *'absence makes the heart grow fonder'* has some truth to it."

"Um, what exactly does that mean?" Scotty asked.

"He means he wants us to ignore her for a while. Act as if we've given up on wanting her to go back with us. Make friends and spend our time with other people" Kindal clarified.

"Exactly" Jesse smiled. "She'll miss having us around. And hopefully she will come looking for us instead of us having to chase around after her."

"That's a bit of a long shot, don't you think?" Scotty said.

"One that I'm confident will work" Jesse replied with a grin.

He watched as Scotty and Kindal headed in the direction of the village, on their quest to befriend the local pack. But he had other plans for himself. He needed to build up a support team to help him get Lacey back. And the first person on the list of people he needed to win over was Luke, her self-proclaimed protector. As much as Jesse disliked him, he knew that if he didn't get Luke on his side he would never get Lacey back.

Jesse stepped into the woods in the direction he saw Luke and Maggie go earlier.

CHAPTER FOUR

Lacey looked up at the eight foot tall chain - linked fence in front of her. The barbed wire at the top looked dangerous. It took forever to find the restricted area of the mountain that she had been told to stay away from. But knowing that no one had searched the area, she felt compelled to do it herself. She pushed back on her hind legs and prepared to jump over the fence.

As her body soared over the top of the fence, a sharp barb got stuck in the flesh of her back leg and ripped a large gash down to her paw. She howled out in pain and fell to the ground. Within seconds, she shifted into her human form. "Damn it" she yelled and surveyed the damage done to her leg.

A large cut stretched from her inner thigh down past her knee. Blood seeped from the wound, covering her leg in red. Lacey looked around for something to help stop the bleeding. She grabbed a handful of leaves from the ground and rubbed them over her leg.

Within minutes, the bleeding stopped and Lacey watched in amazement as the cut healed itself. Inch by inch, her skin closed over the wound, leaving a faint white scar that went down the length of her leg. She had never seen her body heal itself before. All of the other times she had been injured, her body healed while she was unconscious. It truly was a sight to see. She smiled and rubbed her hand down her leg. "Wow" was all she could say.

After a few minutes, Lacey got to her feet and looked up at the fence that she was going to have to leap over again on her way back home. The idea did not sit well with her, especially when she noticed the ball of white fur that was stuck in the barbs. Her fur. It was proof that she had crossed the line into the forbidden territory. She cussed to herself. There was nothing she could do about it now. She turned away from the fence to face the large expanse of trees in front of her.

She was caught off guard at how normal and beautiful everything looked. The woods on this side of the fence looked exactly the same as the other side. The trees were big, green and healthy. Everywhere she looked she saw life. Trees, bushes, animals. She didn't know what she had been expecting but considering the tragic events that had occurred there, in her mind she had pictured a dark, scary, haunted piece of land. She was surprised at how wrong she was, and at the same time…relieved.

Knowing that Cole's actions years ago hadn't destroyed the beauty of the mountain made her feel good inside.

Unfortunately, the feeling didn't last long. As soon as she thought about him, pain erupted from her chest and spread throughout her body. A small gasp escaped her lips and a tear rolled down her cheek. "Oh Cole, I miss you so much" she whispered.

"What are you doing over there?" A female voice said from behind her.

Startled, Lacey spun around to see Mira staring at her from the other side of the fence.

"This fence is here for a reason, you know. We're not allowed on that side of the mountain" Mira said with her hands planted firmly on her hips.

Lacey turned away from her to look at the woods in front of her once more. She wanted to continue on her search but now that Mira was there, she couldn't. At least not at the moment anyway. She let out a deep sigh and approached the fence. "Is there another way out?"

Mira looked up and saw the fur sticking out from the wire and smiled. "Why don't you get out the same way you got in?" she said, sarcastically.

"You know what, forget it. I'll find my own way out. I should have known better than to think you would help me" Lacey spat and started walking down the length of the fence to search for another way out. She did not want to get herself hurt again trying to jump out, especially not with Mira there.

Over the last few weeks, Mira had been playing the role of wannabe friend a little too thick. And Lacey wasn't buying the act.

"Wait" Mira said and dropped her hands from her hips. "I know how you can get back to this side. A few days ago, I saw Jesse come out through a hole in the fence."

Lacey stopped walking. "Jesse? What was he doing on this side to begin with?"

"I don't know. I was hunting when I caught his scent. I followed the smell and saw him as he came out through a hole near the creek. From the look on his face he was pretty pissed so I didn't stick around to ask what he was doing. I finished my hunt and went home."

Lacey looked deep in thought as she processed the information Mira gave her. She surveyed the woods on her side of the fence. "What's over here?"

"What do you mean?" Mira asked with a confused look.

Lacey turned to face her through the fence. "I mean what reason would Jesse have for being here."

"I don't have a clue, unless maybe he was hunting but…" Mira paused to think back to the day she saw him.

"But what?" Lacey prompted.

"He was in human form and fully clothed. He couldn't have been hunting."

Lacey was silent for a moment as an uneasy feeling crept over her again. Something didn't seem right about Jesse being in the forbidden territory. He had no reason to be there.

"You know, there are a few abandoned cabins and a hunter's lodge over there. Maybe Jesse has been using one of them as his own" Mira said then paused, "come to think of it, I've heard his friend Scotty say a few times that he had no idea where Jesse had been spending his nights. So maybe that's it, he's been sleeping in one of the abandoned cabins."

"But why would he do that when he could just share the cabin that Scotty is using?" Lacey asked.

Mira rolled her eyes. "How the hell should I know that? These people are your friends not mine."

"It just doesn't make sense" Lacey mumbled to herself.

"Yeah, a lot of stuff doesn't make sense around here. Like why Jesse still wants you after you left him for Cole. He obviously has some issues." Mira's voice was laced with sarcasm.

Lacey ignored her comment. "Where is the hole at?"

"It's not far from here. Just keep walking and I'll show you where it is."

They walked side by side with the fence separating them for what seemed like forever. Neither of them said a word until they found the hole. Mira pulled the bushes back from her side and Lacey squeezed through.

"Thanks" Lacey said. The fact that she was still butt naked as she stood in front of Mira should have made her feel uncomfortable, but it didn't. Cole had been right when he told her that with time she would outgrow her discomfort with nudity. Once again, the thought of him made her heart ache. She quickly looked away from Mira so that she wouldn't see the pain on her face.

"What's wrong?" Mira asked. She could sense a change in Lacey's demeanor.

"Nothing" she replied and kept her face turned away.

Mira stared down at the ground with an uncomfortable look on her face. "Look, I know we aren't exactly friends. And you have no reason to confide in me or trust me, but I meant what I said before…I am sorry for what I did to you. And I want us to start over and try to be friends if possible."

Lacey gave her a skeptical look. "Sure you do, Mira. I'm not stupid, you're just waiting for the right moment to try and get rid of me again."

"That's not true. I'll admit that I didn't like you when we first met. I thought you were a weak pampered little princess. And I hated the way Cole was so protective of you. It made me sick. But I've seen your strength. You are a lot stronger than I gave you credit for. And I really would like for us to be friends" Mira said, uneasily.

Lacey still didn't believe her. She had seen enough of Mira's cruel side to know that she could never be trusted, but saying so would probably only make Mira hate her more. The phrase *'keep your friends close and your enemies closer'* came to mind. The idea of having a fake friend that she could keep an eye on was better than having to deal with another unexpected attack from behind.

"Alright, Mira" Lacey said as a plan quickly formed in her mind. "You say that you want to be my friend, then prove it."

Mira looked stunned by the request. "Exactly how do you want me to do that?"

"Help me find out what's going on with Jesse."

Mira smirked, "you want me to keep tabs on your boyfriend? Sorry, but I have better things to do with my time than follow him around."

Lacey's body tensed. "He is *not* my boyfriend!"

"Then why do you want me to keep tabs on him?" Mira asked.

Lacey looked away as she said the words she hated hearing herself say, "because I don't trust him."

Mira's eyes widened. "Really? And here I thought you two were going to live happily ever after now that Cole's gone."

"Shut up!" Lacey yelled, her voice bouncing off the trees. "Cole is not gone! He can't be…he's out here somewhere just waiting for me to find him." Her voice cracked despite how hard she tried to keep it level.

Mira flinched from the loudness of Lacey's voice a second before regaining her composure. "Why are you so sure that he's still alive? Everyone else has accepted his death, why can't you?"

Lacey met her eyes with a heartbreaking glare and answered her question. "Because I still feel him here" she laid her hand over her heart as tears swelled in her eyes. "I can't explain it, I just know he's still alive. He has to be…he wouldn't leave me, he promised that he would always be here for me." She looked away from Mira to wipe the tears from her cheek.

Mira didn't know how to respond to seeing Lacey so distraught and vulnerable. She had never been one to comfort others when they were upset and didn't know how to do it now. She wasn't a compassionate person and never had been. But seeing Lacey with her guard down, gave Mira an opportunity to earn her trust. She rested her hand on Lacey's shoulder and gave a weak smile, "You really do love him, don't you?"

She nodded, "yes, I do…more than even I realized. It took losing him for me to understand how very much I love him." She sighed as memories of her old life suddenly came back to her, memories that she wished she could forget. The loneliness that used to terrorize her was creeping up on her once again. She shook her head to clear her mind and met Mira's eyes. "Before I met Jesse and Cole, I never knew what love was. I didn't have family and friends who loved me and cared about my safety. I was an outcast, a freak who could move things with her mind. Those who weren't terrified of me, wanted to study me. My life and heart were lonely. But my life changed the day I met Jesse and Cole. I thought I loved Jesse, he made me feel something I had never felt before…acceptance. And I think I clung to that more than I should have. But it was Cole, who broke through every defense I put up to protect myself. He's the one that touched my heart and showed me what it's like to love and be loved by someone else. And I can't let that feeling go. I can't give up on him. It hurts too much to even think about it."

Mira nodded in understanding. "Then don't give up. If there is one thing I know about Cole, it's that he's a fighter…just like you." She smiled thinly, "maybe you're right. Maybe he is out here somewhere waiting for you to find him. So don't lose hope. I would offer to help but it seems that I already have another job on my hands…babysitting Jesse" she said with a roll of her eyes.

A stunned expression crossed Lacey's face. "Are you serious? You're really going to keep an eye on him for me?"

Mira nodded, "don't look so surprised, I told you I want us to be friends. Besides, I've been a little curious as to what he's up to as well. I don't trust him either."

Lacey smiled to hide her discomfort. She hated feeling suspicious of Jesse. Even though she wasn't in love with him, she still cared about him and considered him a friend. But she just couldn't get rid of the nagging feeling that he was hiding something from her.

Mira lifted her nose and sniffed the air before looking over her shoulder. "We've got company coming."

Lacey also detected the scents coming toward them. She smiled, "Yep, Maggie and Luke must have followed my scent. I swear I can't get away from those two for more than a few hours before they track me down."

"Well, I should get going. I need to find Jesse and see what he's doing" Mira said and turned to leave.

"Mira" Lacey called out after her, "thank you for helping me."

Mira smiled, "that's what friends do, right?" Without waiting for an answer, she fell to the ground and shifted into her wolf form and ran off.

Lacey quickly shifted into her wolf form as well and took off running in the direction of her cabin. She could hear Maggie and Luke running behind her, trying to catch up. But she wasn't in the mood to talk to them at the moment. She pushed herself to run faster. She ran right past her cabin and through the edge of the village, hoping that the scents of her pack mate's would cover hers.

Confident that no one had followed her, she slowed to a walk. After a quick search, she found one of the many hiding spots around the mountain that she and her pack used to hide clothes in case of emergencies, when they needed to shift from wolf form to human. Lacey shifted and grabbed a tee shirt and pair of jean shorts from a hole in the base of a large tree nearby.

She didn't know whose clothes they were and she didn't care. She got dressed, sat down on the ground by the tree and let out a deep breath before laying her head on her knees. She didn't like running away from her friends but she also didn't want them to see her when she was in one of her depressed moods. And she could feel the depression creeping up on her. Helplessness and loneliness were filling her mind and heart, causing a deep ache in her chest. She tried to force it away. She knew she should be on her feet looking for Cole, she was wasting time by just sitting there, but she was too filled with self-pity to move.

A few minutes later, she lifted her head and wiped the tears from her eyes. She shook her head. The scent coming toward her was not someone she wanted to talk to. Why couldn't everyone just leave her alone for a while?

"You look like you could use a friend. Mind if I join you?" Jesse said as he made his way through the woods toward Lacey.

She let out a deep sigh and tried to keep the annoyance she felt with him following her from her voice. "Actually, I came here to be alone."

Jesse stopped in front of her. He looked hurt by her rejection. "Oh" he said in a low voice and turned around to leave.

Guilt built in Lacey's chest when she saw the look on his face. No matter how confused she was when it came to her feelings for him, one thing she knew for sure was that she didn't want to hurt him anymore than she already had. "You know what, now that you're here, I guess I could use a friend to talk to."

Jesse had his back turned to her. The mock sadness he had displayed a moment ago was gone, replaced by a dark, deceitful smile. He took a second to force his grin away before turning around to face Lacey. He started toward her again. "Are you sure? I don't want to impose on your privacy" he said and sat down beside her, not really giving her the opportunity to change her mind.

"I'm sure" she said with a small smile.

Jesse looked at her. Being near her made him happy. He felt like a giddy little school boy with his very first crush. He reached out to brush her hair back behind her ear. He hated her face being hid from his view.

Lacey shied away from him. "So…um, what have you been up to?" she asked to break the ice between them.

Jesse smiled. "Not much. Just hanging around, visiting with a few people that I grew up with."

"That's nice."

"Not nearly as nice as being here with you."

Lacey looked away. This was exactly why she had been avoiding Jesse over the last couple of days. He made their conversations awkward by talking like that.

"I miss you, Lacey. I spend every minute of every day thinking about you" Jesse said and rubbed his hand gently down the side of her face. He touched her chin and turned her face toward him. "Don't you miss me too?"

For a second, her heart ached at the sadness she heard in his voice. But then it was replaced by anger when his voice echoed in her head *'just drop him!'* His words the night on the cliff came back to her, as they often did whenever she was around him. She pushed his hand away from her face and stood up. "You've got to stop doing this, Jesse."

"Stop what?" he said as he got to his feet. "Loving you? If that's what you want me to stop doing, well I can't." He sighed and ran his hand through his jet black hair. "Don't you understand how much I love you? And I know you love me too, despite what you say."

"Maybe I do still love you…but not the way you think. You're my friend, someone I care very deeply for…but that's it."

"Don't say that!" Jesse said in a thick voice and grabbed her shoulders. He stared at her, his jaw clenched as his nails dug into her flesh. "We are supposed to be together. You and me…forever."

Lacey narrowed her eyes at him. "Let…me…go" she growled in a firm, steady voice.

Jesse eased his grip on her shoulders and took a step back. "I'm sorry. I didn't mean to hurt you."

"I have to go" Lacey said and started away from him. He touched her arm. She stopped and glared at him. The look in his eyes warned her of his next move. He quickly closed the distance between them and cradled her face in his hands. A second before his lips would have touched hers, she pushed him backwards. "Don't" she growled.

"Why not? It's just you and me now. Cole is gone. We can finally be happy."

Lacey narrowed her eyes at him as her anger shot through the roof. "I *was* happy!" she yelled. "I was happy with Cole and then you had to show up and ruin everything. If you hadn't come here he would still be alive" she said in a mean voice.

As soon as the words left her mouth, she couldn't believe that she had said them. It was the first time she'd ever admitted to herself that Cole might actually be dead. The thought made her gasp as pain shot through her chest. She narrowed her eyes at Jesse, "Just leave me the hell alone!"

She turned and ran away, shifting into her wolf to gain more speed. She had to outrun the feelings that were twisting her insides into a muddled mess and making her question whether or not searching for Cole really was futile.

CHAPTER FIVE

After a long run to clear her mind, Lacey was just about to climb the steps of her porch when she caught Maggie and Luke's scents in the air. She stopped and looked toward the woods. Something about the scent they were putting off alarmed her. She darted toward the woods. Within seconds, they skidded to a stop in front of her.

Luke kept looking at her then pointing his nose in the direction that they had come from. Maggie positioned herself behind Lacey and nudged her with her body. When Lacey didn't budge, Maggie stomp her front paw on the ground and snorted angrily before running off through the woods.

Lacey finally got the hint and took off after her with Luke falling into step behind her. They ran for what seemed like an hour before Maggie finally skidded to a stop. Lacey nearly ran right into her. She looked at Maggie with questioning eyes and tried to figure out what was going on. Why had she stopped? What did they want her to see?

Question after question popped into Lacey's mind as she looked around expecting to see something that would require her attention. But all she saw was more of the same that she saw everywhere on the mountain…woods. Her gaze flickered back and forth between Maggie and Luke, waiting for one of them to show whatever they wanted to show her or shift and say something. When they both just stared at her with wide eyes, Lacey shook her head and shifted into her human form, which she hated doing in front of Luke.

"Okay, what is so damn important that you two drag me way out here for?" She looked around once more, "I don't see anything."

Luke gave Maggie a subtle nod before turning to leave. He didn't go far, just far enough so that the women could have some privacy. He knew the conversation they were about to have was going to be emotional and figured it was best to let Maggie handle it on her own. He knew how much Lacey hated for others to see her weak side.

Once Luke was out of sight, Maggie shifted into her human form. Lacey had her arms crossed over her chest as she waited for an explanation. But before Maggie could say anything, something caught Lacey's attention. She dropped her arms to her side. Her face went completely blank as she took in a deep breath, catching the subtle traces of a scent she knew all too well. Her eyes grew wide as she stared at Maggie.

Maggie wanted to say something, to tell Lacey why she had brought her there. But one look at her face and she knew that she didn't need to. Lacey brushed past her in a desperate attempt to find the source of the scent assaulting her nose and making her terrified of what she was about to find. She lifted her nose in the air and sniffed again and again. She fell to her knees and began searching through the fallen leaves, shakily digging her nails into the earth.

The more she searched, the stronger the scent became. She followed it over to a pile of broken tree limbs. She jumped to her feet, adrenaline pumped through her veins while fear punched another hole in her heart. Her eyes landed on a thin tree limb sticking out from the pile, she reached out to touch it. The long black hairs stuck on the end of it made her heart almost leap from her chest. She pulled the hairs loose from the dark substance that glued them to the branch. Blood. It smelled like blood. Cole's blood.

The thought sent Lacey back to her knees. She looked up at Maggie with tear-filled eyes as she rubbed the hair between her fingers. "This is Cole's hair" she whispered through the lump in her throat.

Maggie knelt down beside her. "I know" she said softly.

A flood of emotions crossed Lacey's face as she stared down at the hair. Maggie hoped that she could keep her calm so that her powers wouldn't surface. But that hope didn't last long. She felt the power as it built up inside Lacey, making her body vibrate. Maggie rested her hand on her shoulder and gave her a concerned look, "are you alright?"

Lacey squeezed her eyes closed and took a deep breath to force her powers back, but it wasn't easy. Finding Cole's hair matted with his blood terrified her, which in turn, triggered her powers. She stayed like that for several minutes with her eyes closed, taking in and releasing deep breaths. When she finally opened her eyes, Maggie saw the toll their discovery had taken on her.

Lacey's eyes were the saddest Maggie had ever seen. They looked as if the life had been ripped right out of them. Nothing but pain stared back at her. She reached out to hug Lacey but she shook her head and fell back on her butt. She wouldn't take her eyes off the hair in her hand.

Maggie had hoped letting Lacey know about their discovery, would make her feel better about the possibility that Cole was indeed still alive somewhere, instead it seemed to have the opposite effect.

"Lacey" Maggie said, gently, "It's just his hair, nothing more. His body isn't here. So there is still hope that he's alive. Okay."

Lacey lifted her face from the hair and met Maggie's eyes, tears rolled down her cheek. "He *was* alive. He survived the fall. All this time, I was right" she choked out.

Maggie looked over her shoulder for Luke. She was having second thoughts about being the one to deliver the next piece of information that she knew might send Lacey over the edge and make her lose control of her powers. But Luke was nowhere in sight. Maggie let out a deep breath before speaking. "Lacey, there's more that you need to know."

Lacey brought Cole's hair to her nose and inhaled deeply. She knew Maggie was talking to her, but she was too lost in thought to pay attention.

"He wasn't alone when he came through here" Maggie said in a low voice.

Lacey's head snapped in her direction. "What!"

Maggie got to her feet and stood beside the branch where Cole's hair had been found. The branch was even in height with her chest, and at a little over five foot tall, that meant the branch was around four feet from the ground. She pointed to the branch as she looked at Lacey. "Cole is over six feet tall, if he walked through here on his own, injured or not, his hair would have gotten caught on one of the higher branches." She paused to give Lacey the chance to catch on to what she was saying.

When Lacey's eyes widened, Maggie knew that she understood. "Someone was carrying him?" Lacey said with disbelief. She got to her feet and touched the branch, then sniffed it to try and detect another scent, but there wasn't one. Too much time had passed.

Her mind raced with the possibilities of what could have happened to explain Cole's hair and blood being on a branch so low to the ground. But there wasn't one. The only explanation that made sense was that someone had carried him through the woods. Knowing that someone had found him alive and kept him from her, filled Lacey with so much rage that she was tempted to let go of the hold she kept on her powers. She could feel them fighting against her, wanting to take over. But she forced them back and summoned her wolf. She could feel her just under the surface, waiting to be released.

"Who do you think it was?" Maggie asked.

"I don't know" Lacey responded, "but I'm going to find out. And when I do, the person or people responsible for taking him better pray that I never find them. Because if I do…well, let's just say they won't live long enough to regret it."

Maggie watched speechlessly as Lacey shifted into her wolf form and ran off into the woods. After seeing the look on her face, Maggie couldn't help but think that something very bad was about to happen on the mountain. She called out to Luke before dropping to the ground and taking off after Lacey.

*****

Lacey was so upset that she couldn't think straight. She pushed herself to run as fast as her legs could carry her. Everything that she passed blurred together, making her unsure of where she was going. But she didn't care. Her mind was a jumbled mess as she thought about everything that had happened since the night of the fight on the cliff. Someone had lied to her. Someone knew where Cole was and they were keeping them apart. But who?

The possibilities were endless. No one liked Cole. He had told her on many occasions that he had a lot of enemies. She'd even met a few of them when they came to the cabin looking for him. Thinking about Tate and his friends who had attacked her, made her think of Dallas, Tate's cousin.

Dallas had tried to start a fight with Cole at the bonfire. He had threatened him. And even though Jeremiah warned him to leave Cole alone, Lacey never believed that he wouldn't come after him again. Maybe he was the one who had found Cole and was now keeping him hidden somewhere. A fierce growl built in Lacey's throat at the thought. She quickly changed direction and headed for the village with only one thought in mind…to get the truth from Dallas no matter what she had to do to get it.

Half an hour later, Lacey stepped from the trees into the clearing known as the village. The six cabins spaced throughout the clearing had many uses. The school cabins were where Maggie worked as a teacher. And her friend Dean worked at the small store housed in the cabin closest to where she stood.

The smallest of all of the cabins was where the pack doctor, Wilford Sims, had his office. Since everyone on the mountain had the ability to heal their own wounds, the doctor's duties pretty much consisted of delivering babies, bracing broken bones so that they healed correctly, and dealing with Lacey whenever her powers drained her.

Lacey kept her eyes open and alert as she searched her surroundings. There were several people out walking around, some talking on the porch of the school cabin, some going in and out of Dean's store. But everyone was in human form, except for her. She kept her nose low to the ground and tried to detect the whereabouts of the only person she was interested in talking to at the moment.

She heard his voice at the same time she caught his scent. Her head snapped up. Dallas was with a group of men coming around the corner of one of the school cabins. He was a good hundred feet or so away. Lacey took off at a dead run toward him. Before he had a chance to react, Lacey leapt through the air and tackled him to the ground. She dug the claws of her front paws into the flesh of his shoulders and snapped her teeth together mere inches from his face.

The men that were with Dallas stepped back when Lacey looked over at them and growled. Whether they approved of her attacking Dallas or not didn't matter, she was their alpha female.

And they knew about the power she possessed and weren't about to get in her way. Lacey turned her attention back to Dallas and growled once more before shifting into her human form.

She laid on top of him naked, with her arm pushed up against his throat. "Where is he?" she snarled and put more pressure against his windpipe.

Dallas's eyes grew wide as he stared at Lacey in fear. He shook his head from side to side. "Who? Who are you talking about?" he asked, in a rush.

Lacey ground her teeth together and narrowed her eyes at him. She got to her feet and pulled Dallas up by the hair. "Don't play games with me!" she yelled in his face. Her body started to tremble as she balled her hands into fists at her sides.

Dallas looked terrified. He glanced over at his friends for help. But they made no move to help him. "I…I don't know what you're talking about. Who are you looking for?" he stuttered.

Lacey got in his face, he could feel the power radiating off of her. Her hair lifted into the air and blew behind her. The air between them felt electrified as her powers slowly began to surface. "You know damn well who I'm looking for. I'm looking for Cole and you have him hidden somewhere, don't you?" she accused.

Dallas shook his head frantically. "No, no I don't have him. Cole is dead. He's in the river somewhere."

"Liar!" Lacey yelled. She let the hold on her powers slip even more.

Dallas flew backwards into the side of the cabin. The impact was so strong it knocked a hole in the cabin wall, splinters from the wood used to build it scattered through the air as the logs broke. Dallas fell to the ground with blood pouring from his head. Lacey grabbed him around the throat and jerked him to his feet. A crowd gathered around them.

"I don't want to hurt you, Dallas. Just tell me where Cole is and I'll leave you alone" Lacey growled.

Dallas squeezed his eyes closed so that the blood dripping from his head wouldn't get in them. "I don't know what's going on, but I swear I don't have a clue where Cole is" he said weakly.

Lacey was about to use her powers against him again when someone called her name.

"Lacey, what are you doing?"

She looked over her shoulder to see a large group of people watching her every move. Kindal, Scotty, Dean, Jeremiah and Mira were at the front of the group. They looked as if they were preparing to try and restrain her. She looked past them to see the faces of her pack mates, the people she was now in charge of taking care of. The voice that called out to her spoke again. She searched the crowd until she found him. Jesse.

He separated himself from the crowd and started toward her. "What are you doing? This isn't you, Lacey. You don't hurt people. Your heart is too big to do something like this" he said in a gentle voice to calm her down.

Lacey gave him her attention for a fraction of a second before turning back to Dallas. She used her powers to lift him into the air a few feet above the ground.

He screamed and yelled for someone to help him. Jeremiah took a step toward Lacey. She saw the movement from the corner of her eye and shook her head. "Stay out of this, Jeremiah!" she warned.

He stopped and looked nervously at Dallas.

Kindal and Scotty tried next. They moved toward her together. "Lacey, please...you have to get control of yourself.

Someone is going to get seriously hurt if you don't" Kindal said, in a panicked voice.

Lacey let Dallas fall to the ground as she spun around to face her friends. She let out a hysterical chuckle in a voice that didn't sound like her own. "Who says I don't have control? I know exactly what I'm doing? And if you're really my friend, you'll stay out of this."

Kindal flinched at the coldness of her words. This was the side of Lacey that she didn't like to see, the side that scared her. Scotty pushed passed Kindal and stood in front of her to keep her safe in case Lacey lashed out at her. "Lacey, come on let's talk about whatever he did to upset you" Scotty pleaded.

"Go away!" she yelled. The hold she had on her powers was slipping more than she wanted it to. She turned to look at the crowd behind her, "don't make me force you all to leave" she warned in a strained voice.

Most of the crowd quickly dispersed. Only her friends remained. Jesse came up beside Jeremiah and whispered, "What's going on with her? What did this guy do to make her so mad?"

Jeremiah shook his head. "I don't know, but this isn't good."

Mira smirked beside him. She enjoyed watching someone else get the crap beat of them. Especially Dallas, she never liked him anyway.

Lacey was just about to lay into Dallas again when two wolves came running from the woods and took up guard in front of him, blocking her from getting to him. Lacey narrowed her eyes at Maggie and Luke. "Get out of my way" she growled.

Maggie stood up tall and shook her head. Luke mirrored her actions. Lacey stared at them with tears in her eyes. They were her friends and she knew they were only trying to protect her from herself. But right now they were standing between her and the one person who knew where Cole was. She felt conflicted about what she should do. Her upper lip quivered as she tilted her head to the side and pleaded with Maggie to move. "Please get out of the way. I have to make him talk, don't you understand that. He has to tell me what he knows" her voice cracked as she spoke.

Maggie lowered her head slightly and shook it from side to side. It killed her to defy Lacey, but she had no choice. She couldn't stand by and do nothing while Lacey killed Dallas. She glanced over at Luke standing beside her and gave him a nod to leave. He waited by her side for a few seconds then joined his father and the others. He quickly shifted and asked his father for his shirt. With the shirt in hand, he went back to Maggie. She shifted into her human form and put the shirt on. Luke rejoined his father.

"Lacey" Maggie said softly as she took a step toward her, hoping that their friendship ensured her safety. "I know you don't want to hurt anyone. Not even someone as pathetically stupid as Dallas. Let's just go back to your cabin and talk this through. Whatever he did, I'm sure he didn't mean to upset you. Okay."

Tears rolled down Lacey's cheek as an overwhelming sense of despair consumed her. She slowly shook her head. "No. No, Maggie. Don't you see…he's not going to tell me anything unless I make him? I have to do this. I have to hurt him until he talks. Cole is depending on me to find him."

Maggie's face softened as understanding finally hit her as to why Lacey was attacking Dallas. Having missed the beginning of the fight, she had no idea why Lacey was so upset. Now she knew. She inched closer and slowly wrapped her hand around Lacey's. She let out a relieved breath that she didn't get hit with her powers. "It wasn't him, Lacey" she whispered so no one else could hear. "It wasn't Dallas."

Lacey locked eyes with her, searching for any sign that she was lying. But she saw none. All Lacey saw was concern…concern for her. She gasped as the sob she was trying to hold in escaped her throat. She glanced down at Dallas cowering away from her. An immediate sense of regret hit her at the thought that she could have killed him. She threw her arms around Maggie's neck as her body shook with uncontrollable sobs. She wanted Cole. She wanted him so badly that she was losing her mind not knowing where he was at. It was making her crazy.

Maggie wrapped her arms around Lacey and motioned for Luke to help her. Within seconds, he was by her side with a blanket that Dean had retrieved from his store. Luke wrapped the blanket around Lacey as she cried on Maggie's shoulder. Jeremiah and Scotty quickly got Dallas out of sight just in case Lacey decided to finish what she started.

"Let's get you home" Maggie said and started toward the woods with her arm wrapped around Lacey. Luke was on the other side ready to pick her up and carry her if she wanted him to.

Lacey lifted her head from Maggie's shoulder and wiped her eyes. "I'm sorry…I…I didn't mean to lose control. All I wanted was for Dallas to tell me where Cole is."

Maggie frowned, "I know. But he can't tell you what he doesn't know" she said, sadly.

"How do you know he didn't take Cole?" Lacey asked.

Maggie looked to Luke to answer her. "I know it wasn't Dallas because he just came back to the mountain. He left the same night he tried to start a fight with Cole at the bonfire. He said he needed some time to cool off. He just got back this morning. And he didn't even know that Cole was" he paused to think of the best word to use, "missing, until my dad told him earlier today" Luke said.

Lacey looked from Luke to Maggie as their news registered in her mind. She dropped her head low and shook it from side to side. "That means I almost killed an innocent man" she whispered.

"You didn't know" Maggie said, to comfort her.

"That's not an excuse. No one is safe around me, are they? I'm turning into a monster" Lacey said and pulled away from Maggie. She looked around to see Kindal, Scotty and Jesse watching her from the porch of the school cabin. They were her friends but even they were afraid to come near her.

"All that matters now is that we know for sure that Cole *is* out there somewhere" Luke said and glanced toward the trees. "We have to find him."

"And we have to do it on our own" Maggie added.

Luke nodded in agreement. "We don't know who took him or who we can trust. If whoever took him finds out that we're onto them, they might kill Cole before we have a chance to find him."

Lacey's body tensed. "Then we'll make damn sure no one knows what we're doing." She glared across the clearing at her pack members as they went about their business. One of them knew where Cole was. Her eyes shifted from person to person to see if she could tell who the betrayer was. Her mind whirled with the possibilities. So many people stood out, some more than others.

Suddenly a thought popped into her head. Something that she hadn't even considered until that moment. She grabbed Luke's arm, "have there been any unusual scents in the area? Scents from outsiders?" she asked, in a rush.

Luke and Maggie looked alarmed as they took in Lacey's frantic expression. "No, I don't think so. Why?" Luke asked.

Lacey released his arm and let out a deep breath. "Zack. He got away the night that I killed Sasha. He and Cole got into a fight but his body was never found either. Maybe Cole didn't kill him. I mean, I don't know…they disappeared into the woods. I didn't see what happened and Cole never got the chance to tell me whether or not he killed him." She paused to think, "If Zack did get away he could have come back the next day. He could have found Cole and took him somewhere. Maybe he's not even on the mountain anymore."

Luke nodded. "That is a possibility but I don't think that's what happened. If Zack had come back, we would have known. Someone would have caught his scent. That's how we found you the night Jesse tried to take you. We were at the bonfire waiting for you and Cole when we caught the scents of newcomers. We all know Zack's scent now and I can honestly say that I don't think he's been back since that night."

Lacey was quiet as she considered what Luke said. She knew he was right. It was a long shot that Zack was the one responsible, but it was better to believe that it was him than someone from her pack.

"Come on, we can finish this discussion back at your place. We shouldn't be talking about this out in the open. Besides, the sun is starting to set. It's getting late" Maggie said and urged Lacey forward.

The three of them entered the woods on their way to Lacey's cabin. Moments later, they stopped when they heard footsteps coming behind them. They all knew who it was before they turned around to face him.

"What do you want?" Luke asked, coldly.

Jesse ignored him and looked at Lacey, cautiously. His eyes met hers. "I just wanted to make sure you were alright."

"I'm fine" she said and dropped her eyes to the ground.

Jesse stepped closer and eased his hand around hers, ignoring the small growl coming from Luke. "Can we talk? Privately" he asked.

Lacey tensed at the feel of his hand against hers. There was a time when holding his hand was one of the best feelings in the world, now it just didn't feel right. She tried to casually wiggle her hand free of his grip but he tightened his grip. "Not now. I need to stay away from everyone for a while so I can get my head straight." She was still pissed at him.

"I just want to apologize about earlier. It will only take a minute, promise. I'll walk you to your cabin and we can talk along the way."

"I don't think so" Maggie said with a serious look on her face. "She is in no condition to deal with *you* right now."

Jesse ignored Maggie and stared at Lacey. His whole body trembled with the need to kiss her and hold her in his arms. He brushed her hair back behind her ear and leaned his forehead against hers. He knew he was pushing his luck, especially after upsetting her earlier. He felt her body tense up. He hated that his touch didn't have the same effect on her that it used to. "Please Lacey, I just want to talk, that's all."

The sound of his voice pleading with her broke her resistance. She did still care about him even after their argument. She looked at Maggie and Luke, "I'll meet you at the cabin" she said and quickly looked away when she saw the look of disapproval that flashed across Maggie's face.

"What! No, I don't think this is a good idea. You should come with us" Maggie said, her voice full of shock.

"I'll be fine" Lacey said, with a small smile. She felt uncomfortable asking them to leave and she didn't really want to do it, but Jesse seemed desperate to talk to her. "We'll be right behind you."

Maggie's eyes grew wide as she shook her head. She opened her mouth to argue but Luke cut off whatever she was about to say. "Alright Lacey, if that's what you want, we'll meet you at the cabin" Luke said.

Maggie glared at him angrily. He gave her a wink and squeezed her hand. "She'll be fine" he said to calm her. Then he turned his attention to Jesse, "right Jesse, Lacey will be fine with you because if she isn't, you're going to have one hell of a problem on your hands. Do we understand each other?" The threat in his voice was unmistakable. Cole's attitude and protectiveness had definitely rubbed off on him.

Jesse glanced over at Luke, his jaw tight as he spoke, "Yeah, we understand each other. But just so you know, Lacey has never been in any danger from me."

He looked at her and said his next words, "I love her. More than anything in the world."

Lacey looked away, unable to meet his eyes knowing that she no longer felt the same way about him. She pulled the blanket tighter around her shoulders. "Alright then, it's all settled." She looked at Maggie, "I'll meet up with you at the cabin in a little bit."

Maggie's arms were crossed over her chest in a stubborn gesture. "Fine" she snapped and stepped between Lacey and Jesse. She leaned close to Lacey's ear and whispered, "I really hope you know what you're doing."

Lacey cringed at the coldness of her words. She had a feeling that Maggie had the wrong impression about why she wanted to talk with Jesse. Ever since she learned about Lacey's past with him, Maggie had been adamant that he stay away from her. She gave Maggie a weak smile, "I do…trust me, okay."

Maggie quickly turned on her heels and stormed off with Luke right behind her. Lacey could hear her yelling at him in a hushed tone as they walked away. "Why did you let that happen? Why did you say it was okay to leave her with him?"

Lacey and Jesse stayed quiet until they could no longer hear Maggie and Luke's voices arguing with each other.

Once silence filled the air, Jesse raised his brows and said, "Your friend doesn't like me, does she?"

"She's just very overprotective, that's all" Lacey said and started walking in the same direction her friends went. Jesse looked at her hands holding the blanket tight around her body. He wanted to feel her skin against his again, even if only for a second. Instead, he stuck his hands in the front pockets of his jeans and walked close beside her.

Neither of them said anything for a few minutes, until Jesse finally the broke the silence. "I really am sorry about what happened earlier. I didn't mean to upset you."

"It's alright. I guess I could have handled the situation better. But to be honest I think we both have some serious anger issues" Lacey said.

Jesse nodded in agreement, a small smile played on his lips. "Yeah, I think we do too. Although, I have to say, I think yours is a little worse than mine."

They both laughed a little before silence filled the space between them once again. Lacey could tell that Jesse had something he wanted to say. She looked at him with raised brows, "what's on your mind?"

He glanced at her then turned his attention forward as they continued their walk. He knew what he was about to say was more than likely going to start another argument but he couldn't help himself. "I was just wondering how much longer you're going to keep running yourself into the ground searching for a lost cause."

"What's that supposed to mean?"

"It means you're running yourself ragged searching for something that you're never going to find."

Lacey stopped walking and turned to face him with an accusatory look in her eyes. "How do you know that I'm never going to find him?"

"Because it's been almost two weeks. His body or what was left of it after the fall is long gone by now, the river washed it down stream. The sooner you accept that, the quicker you'll be able to move on with your life" Jesse said. He reached out to touch her face, but she jerked out of his reach.

"I'm not having this conversation with you, Jesse. I've told you before that I'm not moving on. Without Cole there is nothing to move on to. And if this is what you want to talk about then I think I'll just catch up with Maggie and Luke" she said and started walking again.

Jesse grabbed her arm to stop her. She looked at his hand around her upper arm then narrowed her eyes at him. He instantly dropped his hand and shook his head sadly. "What happened to us? Where did all this distance between us come from?" he said, and waved his hand between them. "Why is it so hard for us just to spend a few minutes alone with each other? It didn't use to be like this."

Lacey's face softened a bit. "Things have changed Jesse, you know that. I'm sorry that I've hurt you but what we had is in the past. And I think the sooner *you* accept that, the quicker *you* can move on" she threw his words back at him.

Jesse's body stiffened. "What did Cole say to you that made you not want me anymore?"

Lacey stared at him. The change in subject caught her off guard but gave her an opportunity to get some of the answers she'd been waiting for. "My feelings have nothing to do with what Cole told me. But since you asked, he did tell me about what happened with your father. About how he died. And who was responsible."

"You already knew how my father died and who was responsible…the hunters that shot him. I told you that" Jesse said and threw his hands up in the air. "What does that have to do with me?"

Lacey closed her eyes and let out a deep breath before opening them again. Her eyes caught Jesse's and held his gaze as she spoke, "I know, Jesse…I know the truth about what happened. I know that you paid the hunters to kill your father. You had an innocent man murdered."

Jesse's eyes widened. He balled his hands into fists at his sides as his entire body went rigid. "What!" he yelled. "Is that what that bastard told you?"

Lacey held her head high and stood straight, unaffected by Jesse's threatening posture. "Are you denying it? Please don't lie to me. I think after everything that's happened since I met you, I deserve to know the truth."

Jesse just stared at her for what seemed like an eternity. Lacey held his gaze waiting for him to respond. When his body relaxed and he dropped his eyes to the ground she knew he was ready to talk. She took a step toward him and rested her hand on his arm to encourage him to open up. "Why? Why did you do it?" she asked, with true curiosity.

Jesse shook his head at the realization that his worst nightmare had come true. He never wanted Lacey to know what he had done all those years ago. He never wanted her to look at him the way she was now…like she was ashamed of him. The disgust in her eyes made him mad. "My father was *not* an innocent man. He got what he deserved and so did Cole. And that's all I have to say about it" Jesse said coldly. Realizing that his anger made him say something he shouldn't have, he tensed up.

Lacey opened her mouth to speak but Jesse cut her off. "I'm sure you can make it the rest of the way home on your own. I'm not in the mood for talking anymore" Jesse blurted out. Without giving Lacey a chance to respond, he spun around and stormed back in the direction of the village.

Lacey stared at his back as he walked away from her. She was more convinced now than ever that he was hiding something from her. And knowing that upset her very much. She ran the rest of the way to her cabin alone. The dark feelings that swelled inside her as she replayed Jesse's words over and over in her mind - *my father got what he deserved and so did Cole* - made her feel even more unstable than she had already felt.

CHAPTER SIX

Cole grunted from the strain of exercising his legs. He was getting better at bending his knees and his legs were getting stronger, as was the rest of his body. He grabbed ahold of the chains around his wrist above his head and pulled himself into a sitting position on the bed. His body still ached in places but he ignored the pain as he turned around on the bed and faced the wall behind the bed.

The plan that he had been working on played out in his mind and he decided to put it into action. He braced his legs against the frame on both sides of his chained hands. He then leaned back, pulling against the chain, using his legs as leverage. He put all the strength he had into trying to break the chain free of the frame.

His teeth ground together as his jaw clenched tightly. Beads of sweat formed on his forehead and the muscles in his legs ached from the strain, but nothing happened. The chain didn't break. Cole growled out loud in frustration and jerked against the chains in a wild, frantic tantrum. He kicked the frame over and over again. Just when he was about to give up, he heard a small snapping sound. His eyes lit up at the possibility that his freedom was closer than he thought.

*****

Mira kept a good distance back so that Jesse wouldn't catch her scent and know that she was following him. She moved soundlessly from tree to tree for cover. When Jesse stormed back to the village after running off after Lacey, Mira knew that she had to follow him. And now, she was glad that she did.

She dared a glance around the tree in front of her. Jesse was about a hundred feet away. She could tell from the way he was stomping heavily and hitting and kicking things in his path that he was pissed. Every few seconds he looked around to make sure he was alone.

Once Mira realized where he was going she stayed further back, allowing more distance between them. When the fence Lacey had crossed over came into view, she crouched down low to the ground and watched as Jesse made his way through the same hole in the fence that she'd seen him come out of before. "Where the hell are you going" she said to herself and watched him slink off into the woods on the other side of the fence.

Mira made her way through the hole and tried to keep sight of Jesse. He moved at a quick pace and she had to hurry to catch up to him. Her talents as a stealthy hunter definitely came in handy when trying to avoid being noticed. She stayed well hidden and far enough away so that her scent wasn't detectable as she followed Jesse deeper into the forbidden territory.

When he stopped in front of a big pile of what looked like bushes and broken tree limbs, Mira hid behind a tree and watched curiously as he began moving the debris. Her eyes widened when she saw what was hidden behind the blanket of foliage. Jesse was standing in front of an old cabin. Mira ducked behind the tree when he looked over his shoulder to check the woods around him again.

Mira held her breath and hoped that he didn't see her. After a few tense seconds, she heard the door to the old cabin squeak open. She peeked around the tree to see that Jesse was nowhere in sight. She let out a relieved breath and moved closer to the cabin. She knew if she got too close Jesse would know that she was there but she just had to see what he was doing.

*****

Cole kicked at the bed frame one last time before letting his legs fall to the bed. He heard the front door of the cabin ease open and he quickly turned around on the bed and laid down. Jesse's scent filled the tiny space as he stomped through the cabin.

All of a sudden, the door to the bedroom broke from its rusted hinges and flew across the room.

Cole stared at Jesse as he stood in the doorway with his hands braced on either side of the doorframe with his head hung low and his black hair covering his eyes. Cole could sense the anger raging inside Jesse and knew that he was in trouble. He didn't know what had happened but something or someone had set Jesse off and now he was going to be the one who had to pay for it.

Jesse raised his head and glared at Cole before entering the room. His eyes were cold and scary as he made his way over to the bed. "You stupid son-of-a-bitch! Why did you tell her about what happened to our father?" he yelled and landed a punch to Cole's jaw.

Before Cole could respond, Jesse punched him again. "You ruined everything! You're just like that worthless bastard of a father we had."

Cole's head rolled to the side from the impact. His jaw clenched tightly and he turned his face back to Jesse. "What's wrong, Jesse? Is your past coming back to haunt you? Lacey had a right to know the truth. After all, you made damn sure to tell her everything you could about me, didn't you?"

Jesse growled and hit him again. Blood poured from Cole's nose, over his lip and into his mouth. He spit out a mouthful and laughed. "So I take it that there's a little trouble in paradise with Lacey, huh?"

Jesse pulled his fist back to punch him again. Cole growled out loud, his nostrils flared as he narrowed his eyes at Jesse, "Hit me again and I'll rip your damn arms off!" he threatened through tight lips.

A huge grin crossed Jesse's face. He dropped his fist to his side and raised his brows tauntingly. "I'd like to see you try. You seem to forget that I'm the one in control here, not you." In the blink of an eye, he raised his fist once more and struck Cole in the face.

Without thinking, Cole reacted. He grabbed the chains around his wrist and jerked himself into a sitting position and swung his legs out toward Jesse. Catching him off guard, Cole kicked him in the stomach and sent him flying backwards into the wall. Stunned, Jesse jumped to his feet and charged toward the bed.

Cole continued to use his legs to defend himself as Jesse tried to get close to him. He managed to stand up on the bed but the chains prevented him from reaching his full height. They kept his hands pulled down below his waist. But Cole didn't let that stop him from trying his best to get his legs around Jesse. The only thought that ran through his mind was an image of his legs wrapped around Jesse's throat as his body lay lifeless on the floor.

Cole's thoughts were interrupted when Jesse caught the leg that he swung at him and twisted it. Cole yelled from the pain of his bone breaking again. He quickly kicked his other leg out and hit Jesse in the chest. Jesse stumbled backwards, releasing a string of profanities.

"Come on! Let's finish this now!" Cole snarled and jerked against his chains. He spared a brief glance down at his legs, his right one was useless. He could see the bone protruding above his ankle. He ground his teeth together and pushed past the pain. "Now is the best chance you are ever going to get to kill me Jesse, because one way or another I will find a way out of here and when I do you're a dead man."

Jesse's body tensed as he prepared to attack. As he lunged forward, a new scent brought him to an abrupt halt. His head snapped toward the open doorway of the room at the same time Cole's did. Mira was standing in the cabin a few feet from the door with a shocked look on her face. Her eyes darted from Jesse to Cole as understanding hit her. She saw the chains on Cole's wrist and the blood on his face. He looked haggard and extremely malnourished.

"Mira! I never thought I'd say this but I'm so happy to see you" Cole said, with a rushed breath. He looked past her to see if anyone else was with her. A sinking feeling filled his stomach when he realized that she was alone.

Mira locked eyes with Jesse and snarled, "What the hell is going on here?" She didn't wait for him to answer. She turned her attention back to Cole, "we thought you were dead" she shook her head, "Lacey was right, all this time, she was right."

"No, she wasn't" Jesse spat. His hands balled into fists. "My brother *is* dead or at least he will be before she ever finds him."

Mira lifted her upper lip and growled. "We'll see about that. When Lacey finds out about this" she waved her hand between Jesse and Cole and around the cabin, "I have a feeling that *you're* going to be the one that isn't alive much longer."

"Run, Mira!" Cole yelled as Jesse charged toward her.

Mira dropped to the floor on all fours in her wolf form and darted out the door of the cabin. Jesse did the same and ran after her. She ran as fast as she could, dodging trees in her path as she tried to find her way back to the fence. But since she didn't pay much attention to her surrounding when she followed Jesse to the cabin, she didn't know how to go back the way she came. She could hear Jesse running behind her, his scent was getting closer.

Mira leapt over a cluster of rocks in her way that she didn't remember seeing before. Her eyes darted around frantically searching for the fence that would get her to safety but it was nowhere in sight. She began to panic, she was lost and didn't know how to get to the others to warn them about Jesse. The sound of water caught her attention.

Knowing that the fence was near a creek, she changed course and ran toward the water. After a couple thousand feet or so, the fence came into sight. Mira glanced over her shoulder to see that Jesse was right on her heals. She pushed herself to run faster but it wasn't enough. She felt the extra weight on her back and the burning sensation in her neck before she realized what had happened. Her legs gave way beneath her and she fell hard to the ground.

Jesse increased the pressure of his bite on the nape of her neck as his body slid off her back and onto the ground beside her. Mira struggled to free herself but his hold was tight. The pain of his bite was excruciating. Jesse got to his feet with her neck still in his mouth and swung her body against a nearby tree. Her head banged hard against the solid wood. Jesse released his hold and let her body fall to the ground when her eyes closed and she lost consciousness.

Once Jesse was certain Mira was no longer a threat, he shifted into his human form and looked down at her as her body shifted as well. Blood covered her face and neck. Jesse stood over her with his hand braced against a tree and tried to figure out what to do with her. When he heard a small noise from the woods on the other side of the fence, he reacted. He quickly picked Mira up and threw her over his shoulder and ran back to the cabin, hoping that no one had seen him.

Cole was checking on his broken leg when he heard the door of the cabin open again. He tensed when he caught Jesse's scent...and Mira's. He sat up straight when Jesse walked in carrying Mira's motionless body. If it wasn't for the fact that he could hear her heart still beating in her chest, he would have thought she was dead.

"What the hell did you do to her?" Cole yelled.

"None of your business" Jesse said and laid Mira down on the floor by the wall.

Cole shook his head. "You're really screwing up, Jesse. I guess having me want to rip you apart isn't enough. Now you're going to have Jeremiah on your ass too. You better believe he will come looking for her and when he does, all of this will be over for you."

"Just shut the hell up!" Jesse yelled in frustration as he ran his hand through his hair roughly. He looked down at Mira for several minutes. Then as if his mind was made up about something, he nodded to himself. "Alright" he muttered and stomped across the room to the tiny closet in the corner.

He opened the door and pulled out another chain like the one he had on Cole. He grabbed Mira by the hands and dragged her over to the foot of the bed and wrapped the chain around her wrists and ankles before securing it to the metal post at the foot of the bed with an old-fashion lock.

"Jesse, don't do this. Just let Mira go before it's too late" Cole pleaded. As much as he disliked Mira, he didn't want her to get hurt or worse killed. He knew it would destroy Jeremiah to lose her. And he didn't want to see his cousin in that kind of pain. They didn't always get along but Cole did care about him.

"I told you to shut up!" Jesse growled and reached for Cole's legs. Before Cole had the chance to move them out of the way, Jesse threw a chain around his ankles.

Cole tried to fight against him but the pain that assaulted him every time he tried to move his broken leg was too much. He did manage to get in one good kick to Jesse's face with his good leg before Jesse got the chains secured around his ankles.

"Damn it" Jesse spat and grabbed his nose. Blood seeped through his fingers and rolled down his arm. "Bastard!" he said and landed a quick punch to Cole's stomach as he laid down flat on the bed. Cole gasped from the pain and tried to double over but couldn't move with his legs and wrists chained.

Jesse wiped the blood from his hand on the mattress and grabbed Cole's face in his hand. He squeezed his jaw hard and forced Cole to look at him. "You're going to regret that little move because this hate-hate relationship that we have going on is about to come to an end" he smiled, blood covered his lips and teeth. "You see, you might have caused a little bump in the road between me and Lacey by telling her about our father, but she still loves me. I came here to let you know that we're going to be mated *tomorrow*. As a matter of fact, she's with Maggie right now planning the ceremony."

Cole's nostrils flared and his eyes narrowed into slits. He tried to jerk his face from Jesse's grip as he gritted words out through tight lips. "No! You can't…"

Jesse smiled again. "Yes, we can and we are. Lacey loves me, not you. She's already forgotten all about you, don't you get that? You heard Mira…Lacey thinks you're dead. She's moved on. She never really loved you to begin with. You were just a substitute until we found our way back to each other" he paused to savor the look of total devastation on Cole's face. "And just like I promised you, brother, your agony will end as soon as Lacey and I are mated."

Jesse dropped his hand from Cole's face and turned to leave. He checked Mira's chains to make sure they were secure before turning his attention back to Cole, who was unusually quiet. "What? No threats? No snarky comebacks…nothing? I expected more from you than that" Jesse said, with satisfaction. "I at least expected to hear again how you intend to kill me." He waited for Cole to say something…but he didn't. Instead, he just closed his eyes and turned his head away.

Jesse gave him a serious look. "Too bad you couldn't have just looked the other way when all this first started. If you hadn't taken Lacey away from me, none of this would be happening right now. This is your fault not mine. You should never have tried to come between us, because now instead of living your worthless life hunting and killing, you're going to die. You should have minded your own damn business and stayed out of mine."

Cole kept his eyes squeezed closed as his heart shattered into a million pieces. Knowing that in twenty-four hours Lacey was going to be lost to him forever caused every fiber in his body to ache and made him wish for the death that Jesse kept promising him was coming.

Jesse left without saying another word. Once outside of the cabin he made sure to cover the door completely before flopping down on the ground with his arms resting on his knees. So much had happened in the last couple of hours and he wasn't sure what to do next. The plan he had in the beginning was quickly coming unraveled and now he had complicated things even more by kidnapping Mira. Things were getting out of control.

Jesse punched the ground beside him in aggravation. Nothing was working out the way he planned. His plan was simple…get Lacey to fall back in love with him and become his mate then kill Cole. He had it all worked out perfectly in his mind but in reality his plan was rapidly falling apart.

He was nowhere close to getting Lacey back. And while he did enjoy torturing Cole with all the lies he'd been telling him about how in love he and Lacey were, this time his lie had created a deadline. He now had one day to convince Lacey to become his mate or Cole would know that he had been lying. And to add to his problems, now he had to figure out what to do with Mira.

As Jesse sat there on the ground thinking, he was momentarily stunned by the predicament he was in. Once again he was shocked by the things he was doing. But he quickly pushed the feeling aside. He had come too far to turn back now and he had no intention of ever letting Lacey know what he had done with Cole. Right or wrong, he had to follow through with what he started. He got to his feet feeling more determined than ever to win Lacey back.

He looked at the mound of bushes in front of him that hid the only evidence of the kind of man he truly was within it and he knew what he had to do. He was tired of playing games with Cole and dragging out the inevitable. As long as Cole was alive, there was a possibility that someone would find him and ruin everything. Jesse couldn't let that happen. It was time to get rid of him once and for all. And Mira too. She was evidence against him.

With his mind made up, he took a step toward the hidden cabin. Just as he started removing the bushes in front of the door, he caught the scents of several of Jeremiah's pack mates in the woods. They were a good distance away, probably hunting on the other side of the fence but Jesse couldn't take the chance of being seen or his scent being detected.

He hastily recovered the cabin door and ran off deeper into the woods so that he could circle around to the other side of the fence without being caught. He promised himself that the next chance he got to come back to the cabin, he would finish what he knew had to be done.

CHAPTER SEVEN

"So what did Jesse want to talk to you about?" Maggie asked Lacey as she stared at her from across the room. She was still ticked off that Lacey had stayed behind with Jesse.

"Nothing" Lacey said and buttoned up the white flannel shirt she had just put on. "You were right. I shouldn't have stayed behind" she sighed sadly before shaking her head, "I really wish I had come home with you and Luke."

Sensing that something was wrong, Maggie crossed the room and stood in front of Lacey with a concerned look on her face. "Why? What did he do? Did he hurt you?" Maggie asked, in a panicked voice and glanced toward the cabin door.

Luke was waiting outside for her to get dressed and Lacey could tell that Maggie wanted to run out and get him. Lacey slowly shook her head. "No Maggie, he didn't hurt me. He would never do that...at least not physically." But he had hurt her with what he said. She sat down in one of the chairs at the table and replayed her conversation with Jesse back in her mind. She looked up when the door opened and Luke walked in.

He smiled when he saw that she was completely dressed. But his smile quickly faded when he saw the worried look on Maggie's face. He immediately went to her. "What's wrong?" he asked.

"I don't know" Maggie said and looked at Lacey. "She hasn't said anything yet."

Maggie and Luke both stared at Lacey waiting for her to talk. She let out a deep breath and told them what was bothering her. "I think...I think Jesse may have something to do with Cole's disappearance...he said something that I don't think he meant to say in front of me. He said that Cole got what he deserved" she sighed, "I saw the look in his eyes when he said it, he meant it."

Maggie and Luke looked at each other, then at Lacey. "Maybe he was talking about Cole falling off the cliff. You know they hated each other. Maybe that's what he meant" Luke said.

Lacey thought about it for a second then she shook her head. "No, that's not what he meant."

"How do you know?" Maggie asked.

Lacey looked at her. "I just do. I can't explain it but I know he's hiding something. I think he found Cole after he fell. But what scares me is …I don't know what he did to him." Her eyes began to water as her voice lowered. "Maybe he killed him. They've been fighting each other their whole lives. If Cole was injured and unable to defend himself, Jesse could have easily killed him. That would explain why he's so adamant that Cole is dead because he killed him." A tear slipped from her eye and rolled down her cheek.

"Oh Lacey, don't think like that" Maggie said and hugged her. She pulled back and wiped the tear from Lacey's face with her hand. "Don't cry, okay. We don't know anything for sure. Maybe Cole is still alive and if he is, we will find him."

"And if we find out that Jesse is responsible for whatever happened to Cole, he'll be sorry he ever came here" Luke said and placed his hand on Lacey's shoulder to comfort her. But nothing either of them said made her feel any better. Because if Jesse had killed Cole, it wasn't him that she held responsible, it was her. She blamed herself. Because until she came into their lives, they had avoided harming each other. If Cole was dead, it was her fault. And that possibility was looking more and more likely.

"Lacey, are you alright?" Maggie asked when she noticed the tortured look on her face. It was clear that bad thoughts were going on in her head.

Lacey closed her eyes and turned her face away. Guilt was eating a new hole in her already broken heart. She could feel her powers trying to get out. She was hurting and her guard was down. The control she had over her powers was slipping. The table and chairs began vibrating against the floor.

Maggie shot Luke a warning glare as they both tensed up. All of the doors on the kitchen cabinets started swinging open and closed on their own. Luke grabbed Maggie's hand, ready to yank her out the door before things got too out of control. She pulled against him and reached her other hand out to Lacey.

Lacey's eyes shot open. "Don't" she said sadly and shook her head at Maggie. Her powers weren't completely out of her control. She knew what she was doing. She desperately needed the release that using her powers offered. All of the pent up anger at herself and the pain in her heart was too much to keep inside. "I don't want you to get hurt, Maggie. Please leave. I...I need to be alone."

Maggie dropped her hand as a sad look crossed her face. "Lacey, don't push us away. Let us help you. You can control your powers, I know you can."

Lacey met her eyes as tears slid down her cheeks. "I don't want control right now. I need to release some of the pain that's choking me to death. And this is the only way I know how to do it. I'm sorry" she said and used her powers to open the cabin door and push Maggie and Luke out onto the porch before slamming the door shut in their faces.

Almost instantly, the sound of things breaking inside could be heard through the door - glass shattered, furniture scraped across the floor and wood splintered. But the sound of Lacey crying was louder than all of that. Maggie reached for the door knob but Luke grabbed her hand to stop her. "We need to give her some time. She's hurting."

Maggie looked at him with tears in her eyes. "I know. I think for the first time since Cole fell off the cliff, she actually believes he might be dead now that she knows Jesse is involved. And it's killing her."

Luke wrapped his arms around Maggie as she began to cry. He knew she was right. Lacey did believe that Cole was gone. He saw it on her face. After two weeks of everyone trying to convince her, she finally believed it. Luke could feel her pain as she screamed from inside the cabin. It was a pain that he hoped he never had to experience.

With a heavy heart, he led Maggie down the steps of the porch and away from the cabin so that Lacey could grieve in private. He just hoped that the cabin would still be standing when he came back to check on her later.

*****

Lacey laid down on the bed and cried her heart out as everything in the cabin swam in the air above her - clothes, pieces of glass that used to be her dishes, splintered pieces of wood that moments ago had been her new dining table and chairs - were just a few of the things hovering in the air.

She had wanted so desperately to believe that Cole was alive somewhere, waiting for her to find him. She had actually convinced herself that as long as she kept looking for him, one day she would find him alive and well. But now, knowing that Jesse was somehow involved, all of that hope was gone. She knew how much he hated Cole and the fact that Jesse was so adamant that he was dead just made everything click together in her mind. He knew because he killed him.

Lacey sat bolt upright in the bed and screamed from the pain of knowing that she would never see Cole again. A burst of power erupted from within her. The entire front half of the cabin exploded outward. Lacey lifted her arm to cover her face as debris from the explosion flew toward her.

After several minutes, she opened her eyes to see that the entire front of her cabin was gone – the kitchen, the porch and the bathroom were all gone. Nothing but piles of broken logs and glass was scattered on what was left of the floor and in the front yard. Lacey looked to the trees surrounded in darkness across the yard as a calm feeling fell over her. The release of her powers was like a warm blanket wrapping around her, comforting her.

She wiped the moisture from her eyes and stared into the night as images of Cole filled her mind. The peaceful way he looked when he slept, the way his eyes softened when he smiled, the devilish charm he had when he teased her. Everything rushed into her at once making her gasp. They were her memories and perhaps the only thing she had left of Cole, and it hurt to know she would never again make new ones.

She laid back down on the bed completely unbothered that her cabin was now open to intruders and animals. All she cared about now was trying to come up with a plan to get Jesse to tell her where he hid Cole's body so that she could give him the proper burial that he deserved before she took her revenge.

The thought of taking Jesse's life caused a new ache in her chest but she forced it away. It might destroy what was left of her heart and her soul but she couldn't let him get away with killing Cole the way he got away with killing his father. She couldn't let that happen no matter what she had to do.

*****

Kindal walked over to the bed and looked down at Lacey as she slept. Dry tear streaks covered her face. Kindal glanced around at what was left of the cabin and shook her head. "What the hell happened here?" she whispered to herself before sitting down on the edge of the bed and resting her hand on Lacey's arm. She said her name twice but using her powers had left Lacey weak and tired. She was in a deep sleep.

Kindal stood up and blew out a deep breath as she surveyed the damage done to the cabin. She started picking up pieces of broken logs that were scattered across the floor in front of the bed and threw them to the yard. Her shock at coming home and finding things the way they were had her preoccupied and she didn't notice she wasn't alone until a voice from the darkness outside the cabin startled her.

"What the hell happened?" Jesse asked as he stepped over a pile of wood and broken logs where the porch used to be.

Kindal looked at him with raised brows. "Those were my exact words when I got here too." She looked over her shoulder at Lacey asleep on the bed then back at Jesse. "Someone must have upset her again but I'm sure it wasn't that Dallas guy. Jeremiah asked Scotty and me to keep an eye on him and he hasn't come near her since she attacked him earlier. We followed him to his friends place and he's been there for the last couple of hours. I got tired of watching him play cards so I came home and this is what I found." She motioned to the missing wall of the cabin.

Jesse walked past Kindal and over to the bed. He leaned over and brushed Lacey's hair back from her face.

"She's been crying" Kindal said from the other side of the bed.

"I can see that" Jesse said and ran his hand down Lacey's cheek. He lowered his head to hers and placed a kiss on her forehead. It was the closest that he had been to her since their last night together in Carol Springs. He let his lips linger on her skin longer than he should have judging from the growls that suddenly filled the room.

Jesse stood up straight and raised his brows at the two light grey wolves standing where the front door used to be. Maggie and Luke both growled again and took a step toward the bed. Maggie kept her eyes on Lacey while Luke shifted into his human form to confront Jesse.

"You need to leave right now!" Luke said as he approached Jesse.

"Why? He didn't do anything to Lacey. This is the way we found her" Kindal said, in Jesse's defense.

Luke glanced over in her direction. "You can leave too. And I'm not just talking about the cabin either. I want you off the mountain." He turned his attention to Jesse, "You're not welcomed here anymore."

"Says who" Jesse replied dryly.

"Says me" Luke said and got in his face. "No one wants you here. And if I ever catch you near Lacey again, I'll make sure your presence here is no longer an issue."

"Is that a threat, Luke?" Jesse asked, with amusement in his voice. His hope of getting Luke on his side quickly faded.

"Take it however you want to, but you better stay away from her. You've done enough damage as it is."

"What's that supposed to mean?" Kindal asked and looked back and forth between Luke and Jesse. "Jesse has never hurt her."

Luke looked at her from the corner of his eye. "Yeah, you keep telling yourself that if it makes you feel better. You have no idea what your friend has done but I do. And I know that the last place he is going to want to be is *here* when Lacey wakes up. Take my advice, leave while you still can."

Kindal gave Jesse a confused look. "What is he talking about?"

Jesse shrugged his shoulders. "How the hell should I know?" he said as he and Luke stared at each other. The tension between them sizzled.

Maggie eased up behind Luke and gave a subtle whine to let him know to back off and not start a fight. He looked down at her for a second then back at Jesse. "You know what, you want to stay here…fine, stay. But Lacey is coming with us. This cabin is no longer suitable for our alpha female anyway." He stepped away from Jesse and scooped Lacey up in his arms and turned to leave.

Jesse started after him. "Wait! Where are you taking her?"

Maggie quickly intercepted him. She stood between him and Luke and growled. "None of your damn business" Luke said. He looked down at Maggie and smiled before meeting Jesse's eyes again. "And if I was you, I wouldn't follow us either. I think Maggie is just dying for a reason to get her teeth into you."

As if in total agreement, Maggie pulled her upper lip back from her teeth and growled again.

Jesse ignored the warning and took a step forward. Maggie growled louder and snapped her teeth at him. Luke had never seen her look so fierce. At that moment she reminded him a bit of his mother.

Kindal put her hand on Jesse's chest to stop him from taking another step. "Just let them go. You can talk to Lacey tomorrow when she wakes up."

Jesse brushed her hand away and turned his back to Maggie and Luke as they left. Once their scents no longer lingered in the air, Jesse turned to Kindal and said, "I'm going to stay here tonight. Go stay with one of the pack females that you were supposed to make friends with."

Kindal looked like she wanted to argue but instead she obeyed his order. Jesse looked down at the bed where Lacey had been sleeping. He ran his hand over the spot that was still warm from where her body had been laying. He laid down and buried his face in the mattress, inhaling the scent she left behind. At the moment it was all he had. Maybe all he ever would have.

CHAPTER EIGHT

Cole knew the exact moment that Mira regained consciousness even though he couldn't see her. The cabin was dark and she was on the floor at the foot of the bed. Her accelerated heart beat told him she was awake. He waited for her to say something. Her chains rattle against the metal foot post of the bed as she pulled against them.

"What the hell?" she said in a rough voice and jerked against the chains again. The chain was so tight around her ankles that she could feel her blood pulsing against her skin.

"Take my advice, don't do that. The chains will dig into your skin and it hurts like hell" Cole said and looked up at his own hands. The chain was halfway embedded into his flesh because he had pulled against it so much. The flesh that was showing was starting to turn black, most likely from infection. But he didn't pay any attention to it anymore.

"What the hell is going on, Cole? Why is Jesse doing this?" Mira asked and struggled against her chains, trying to find a way to free herself.

Cole stared blankly up at the ceiling as he spoke, his voice was dry and tired. "Don't act so surprised, Mira. You know just as well as I do that it was only a matter of time before this feud between me and Jesse took a nasty turn. He saw his chance to get rid of me and he took it. But I'm pretty sure his plan didn't have anything to do with you until now. Looks like you'll be sharing this prison with me, at least until after the ceremony. Then it will all be over. Maybe he won't kill you too, but I don't know" Cole babbled, feeling defeated.

Mira gave up on her chains and leaned her head back against the foot of the bed wishing that she could see Cole so she didn't have to talk to the empty space in front of her. "What the hell are you talking about? What ceremony? Don't tell me Jesse has some kind of sick death ceremony he wants to perform before he kills us. That's just crazy."

Cole closed his eyes and ground his teeth together. "Don't play dumb with me, Mira. I know about the mating ceremony. Jesse told me everything. So there's no need to keep it from me" he said, sadly.

Mira shook her head in annoyance. "Since you seem to know everything why don't you tell me what the hell you're talking about because I don't have a clue? All I know is that you've been missing for almost two weeks and until I followed Jesse here today, I seriously thought you were dead. So if you know more than that please enlighten me with your information."

"I know about Lacey and Jesse's mating ceremony!" Cole yelled. "So stop pretending like you don't know. Lying to me about it only makes it worse. I don't need your sympathy."

Mira laughed out loud. "My sympathy? Cole, you are so damn stupid. Why would you believe anything Jesse tells you? He kidnapped you and has you chained to a damn bed, what makes you think he would tell you the truth about anything?" she shook her head in disbelief, "I swear I don't know what the hell Lacey sees in you. When you first came here I thought she wasn't good enough for you, but now I know your dumbass isn't good enough for her. Do you have any idea what she's been through since you fell over the cliff?"

"My guess is she's been falling back in love with Jesse and planning her mating ceremony" Cole said, in a stiff voice.

Mira rolled her eyes and banged the back of her head against the bed in aggravation. "You're lucky that I'm chained up right now or else I'd kick your ass for being so stupid. Here let me spell it out for you. Lacey…is…not…with…Jesse. I can't believe you thought that. She has spent every day looking for you. Even when everyone else stopped looking and told her that she should too, she didn't." She sighed and thought back to the days following his fall, "when you first went missing, every time anyone said that you were dead she freaked out. She is the *only* person who hasn't given up on you. And here you are questioning her love. When she finds us, I hope she beats the hell out of you. I'll even help her if she wants me to."

Cole listened to everything Mira said, he wanted to believe her. He desperately needed to believe that Lacey still wanted him but after almost two weeks of hearing Jesse explain in detail how things had progressed between him and Lacey, Cole had his doubts. Especially since Mira was the one giving him this new information. She wasn't exactly known for her honesty. "So since when did you become such a good friend of Lacey's? Why should I believe you?"

Mira sighed and pulled against the chains holding her hands over her head. "These damn chains are hurting my arms" she said.

Cole didn't say anything as he waited for her to answer his question. Mira was quiet for a few minutes. "Lacey and I aren't really friends" she finally said. "She doesn't trust me."

Cole shook his head. "What do you expect, you tried to kill her."

"I know" Mira said, in a regretful voice. "I was wrong. I felt threatened by her, okay. I knew she wasn't like us from the first time I talked to her. I could sense the power in her and it scared me. You know me, I've always got to be the best at everything. I knew she was stronger than me even though she didn't know it. I've told her how sorry I am for what I did. I really do want to be her friend. I thought I could earn her trust by doing her a favor and now I'm stuck here with you."

"What was the favor she asked you to do?"

Mira lowered her head as she spoke, "she asked me to follow Jesse. She doesn't trust him either. She knows he's hiding something but I don't think it ever crossed her mind that what he's hiding is you. If she thought that, she probably would have killed him by now."

"Why do you think that?" Cole asked.

"Haven't you been listening? Lacey is so in love with you that she's letting her grief over not knowing where you are or if you're even still alive drive her crazy. I've watched her over the last couple of days. I've seen her break down and cry uncontrollably at the end of a long day of searching when she thought she was alone. And today I saw her walk into the middle of the village butt naked and use her powers to attack Dallas in front of everyone. She damn near killed him. And probably would have if Luke and Maggie hadn't stopped her" she paused, "there is no doubt in my mind if she knew Jesse was holding you captive here, she would kill him. She's just that unstable."

Cole remained silent as he took in everything Mira told him. His heart ached at hearing how distraught Lacey had become. But he needed to hear more about her. He desperately needed a connection to her and at the moment that connection was Mira. He tried to keep his voice from choking up as he spoke, "I see her face every time I close my eyes, she's always smiling."

"Yeah, well she doesn't smile anymore" Mira said in a flat tone.

Cole closed his eyes and remembered the way she had looked the last time they were together at his parent's cabin. She had made all of his dreams come true when she agreed to make the cabin their own so that they could raise a family there. The love and happiness he had felt at that moment came rushing back to him. He ground his teeth together and disregarded his own advice and jerked hard against the chains on his hands. "Damn it! I'm such an idiot. I should have known better. I never should have doubted her."

"It's about time you rejoined the land of reality" Mira said sarcastically. "I'm just going to blame your lack of common sense in believing everything Jesse told you to the fact that you've been starved and beaten so badly. It will be our little secret. But its time you get your head straight now, we have to find a way to get out of here."

Cole let out a half-hearted chuckle. "What the hell do you think I've been trying to do? The chains are unbreakable and my legs are basically useless. They were broken in the fall and didn't heal correctly. When I was finally able to use them again, Jesse re-broke my right leg when we were fighting earlier."

Mira growled in frustration. "There has to be a way out!" She lifted her legs from the floor then brought them back down as hard as she could to try and break the chain against the floor. But all her action did was cause the chain to push into her skin, and make her scream from the pain of it.

Not willing to accept defeat, she continued to hit her legs against the floor as she jerked her hands against the chains around her wrist. She looked like a caged animal as she struggled to get free but nothing happened.

"Stop it, Mira! Don't waste your energy" Cole yelled at her.

"I'm not going to just sit here and wait for Jesse to come back and kill us!" she screamed back at him.

"Neither am I. But we need a plan. You need to calm down so we can think and come up with a way out of this" Cole said in a stern tone.

Mira stopped moving and leaned her head back against the bed. She closed her eyes and let out a deep, calming breath.

"Fine, we'll try it your way. Do you have any bright ideas on how we can get out of these chains?"

Cole was silent for several minutes. All of a sudden his eyes grew wide and a small smile pulled up the corners of his mouth. "Actually, I think I do." He turned his head up so that he could see the metal headboard. He couldn't believe that he had forgotten about the snapping noise he had heard earlier when he was kicking it before Jesse busted in and started beating him.

Cole wrapped his hands around the metal bar and tugged against it using all the strength he had. He could hear a rattling sound like something had come loose.

"What was that?" Mira asked.

"I think I broke something on the frame when I was kicking it earlier" Cole replied. He continued tugging against it then started shaking it. The whole bed shook from the force he was using. A loud cracking sound echoed in the room seconds before the head of the bed crashed to the floor, leaving Cole's upper body suspended in the air a foot above the mattress. The frame under the bed had detached from the headboard, which was still in place and Cole's hands were still chained preventing him from falling with the bed.

He grunted in pain as the weight of his body pulled the chains tighter around his wrists, digging deeper into his flesh. Fresh blood rolled down his arms.

"What the hell happened?" Mira asked and tried to turn her head around to peek over the foot of the bed. From the corner of her eye, she could barely see Cole's feet chained inches away from her face, but that was all she could see. "Are your hands free?" Mira asked, hopeful.

"No" Cole growled, his voice strained. The pain in his arms and legs as his weight pulled against the chains was almost enough to make him scream. But he kept his lips tightly closed.

"Damn it!" Mira yelled, "We're never going to get out of here, are we?" She waited for Cole to say something. When he didn't, she called out his name, "Cole? Cole, are you alright?"

Silence answered her and she began to panic. "Cole…answer me damn it!"

Still nothing. She reached up and grabbed the chains around her wrists and pulled herself up so that she could see over the end of the bed. What she saw caused a lump to form in her throat. Cole was suspended in the air with blood covering his arms. The chains were deeply embedded into his flesh. She listened carefully for his heartbeat. When she heard it, she let out a deep sigh. He had passed out, most likely from the pain or maybe from exhaustion. But he was still alive.

Mira let go of her chain and fell back to the floor and prayed that someone would find them soon or it would be too late to save Cole.

CHAPTER NINE

Light shined through the window onto Lacey's face. Confusion brought her out of sleep. She knew there were no windows near her bed. She eased her eyes open and blocked the sunlight with her hand then sat up in bed and looked around the room. She knew instantly where she was, Maggie's scent was everywhere.

Just as she was getting out of bed, the bedroom door opened and Maggie walked in carrying a tray of food. Seeing her with food was a typical sight Lacey had grown used to. Maggie froze when she saw that Lacey was awake. She smiled before calling over her shoulder, "she's up. You guys can come in now."

Lacey raised her brows in question as Maggie sat the tray of food down on the night stand beside the bed. "Don't worry, it's just Jeremiah and Luke" she whispered.

"Why am I at your cabin? And how did I get here?" Lacey asked as Luke and Jeremiah made their way into the room.

Maggie put her hands on her hips and shot Lacey a chastising look. "Are you serious? Do you have any idea what you did to your cabin last night? We found you asleep on the bed and brought you here. You were out cold. You're lucky we went back to check on you." She didn't think mentioning that they caught Jesse kissing her was a good idea considering Lacey's temper.

Lacey looked embarrassed for a moment then she pushed passed it and grabbed a muffin from the tray. "Thanks" she mumbled before acknowledging Luke and Jeremiah's presence. They both had cautious looks on their faces. "What's going on?" she asked them.

"We need to talk, Lacey" Jeremiah said as Luke stood beside Maggie and wrapped his arm around her shoulder.

"Okay. About what?"

Jeremiah looked uncomfortable as he spoke, "We all know that you're having a hard time right now with everything that happened with Cole and all, but the pack needs you. I know you don't really know what is expected of you yet, Cole didn't really get the chance to explain everything. But without an alpha male, running the pack is left to you. And right now everyone is really stressed not knowing what's going to happen, especially after what you did to Dallas. The pack needs stability, they need a leader. Someone who is involved with the community and who can settle disputes and make sure everyone is safe." He paused to think of the best way to say what he had to say next. "If you don't want the position now that Cole is gone then we need to…"

"No!" Lacey said abruptly, "I am not giving up my position. This is what Cole wanted for me and I'm not throwing it away" she said with conviction. Until that moment she never realized how much she wanted to be the alpha female.

Jeremiah looked startled by her outburst. "Then you are going to have to become more involved with the pack. We're having a cookout in the village today. Everyone thought it would be a good way to ease some of the tension they're feeling. And it will be a good opportunity for you to show the pack that you are ready to be there leader."

Lacey dropped her muffin on the tray and shook her head. She already had plans. She intended to go across the fence again and look around. "I can't. I have other plans for today."

Jeremiah shook his head and ran his hand through his hair. He already knew what her plans were, the same as every other day since Cole's accident, she was going to search for him. "Lacey, you have got to move past this. It's time to accept…"

Maggie quickly interrupted Jeremiah from finishing the sentence she knew was going to upset Lacey. "What Jeremiah means is that it wouldn't hurt to spend a few hours with the pack and afterwards, we will help you with your other plans."

"Yeah Lacey, it's a good idea to take a little break" Luke added.

She looked at each of them before flopping down on the bed. She really didn't want to waste even a few hours mingling with the pack when she still didn't know where Cole was, but as she looked at her friends she knew they weren't going to take no for an answer and they were right.

She needed to take her position more seriously. And the more she thought about it the more she liked the idea. Going to the cookout gave her the opportunity to talk to Jesse again. She needed to find a way to get him to confess what he did to Cole and where he hid his body.

"Alright, I'll go" Lacey said with renewed energy. The huge smile that crossed Maggie's face was the first real smile Lacey had seen on her in a long time.

"Good. You should try to be in the village around lunch time. The cookout will last all day and probably into the night but you don't have to stay that long if you don't want to" Jeremiah said then turned to Luke. "Have you seen your mother lately?"

"Not since yesterday. Why?"

A worried look crossed Jeremiah's face. "She didn't come home last night. I was hoping you'd seen her around."

"The last time I saw her was in the village before we took Lacey home. She probably went to the city to get supplies for the cookout and decided to stay the night like she did the last time. Remember all the crap she brought home. That's why I will never let Maggie go shopping without me" Luke said with a chuckle.

Jeremiah put on a fake smile and nodded. "You're probably right. I'm sure she'll show up later today."

The only problem with Luke's theory was that Mira didn't know anything about the cookout because Jeremiah had just decided to have one that morning. "If any of you see Mira, tell her that I'm looking for her" Jeremiah said before leaving.

He was used to Mira disappearing from time to time. She had done it many times before. But he had already checked her stuff at home and her purse with all of her money was still there. He was starting to get worried but not so much so that he felt something was wrong. He started toward the village to get things ready for the cookout with the hope that Mira would be there.

*****

Lacey could hear music playing from the village as she followed Maggie and Luke through the woods. She decided it was best to go ahead and let them know about her plan to get close to Jesse. She didn't want Maggie to get the wrong idea again when she saw her talking with him. She cleared her throat to get their attention.

"I need to tell you guys something. I don't want you two to flip out if you see things you don't like today" she said casually.

Maggie and Luke both stopped walking and turned around to face her. "What do you mean by that?" Maggie asked.

"Well, you might see me do some things that you aren't going to like" Lacey said sheepishly.

"Like what?" Luke asked and glanced back and forth between Lacey and Maggie.

Lacey took a few seconds to answer him. She knew they weren't going to like her plan since they were both loyal to Cole and considered themselves her protectors, but she didn't see where she had any other choice but to follow her plan to get the information she needed. She blew out a deep breath, "I'm going to flirt with Jesse and I don't know how far I'm going to have to take it."

"What!" Maggie yelled and pulled away from Luke.

"Look, I know this is not what you want to hear and it sure as hell isn't what I want to do, but" Lacey paused, her voice cracked and a lump formed in her throat, "Jesse may be the only one who knows where Cole's body is. I didn't get to him in time to save his life but I can still give him a decent burial." She quickly wiped away the tear that slipped from her eye.

"Oh sweetie, what makes you think Jesse will tell you that? Even if you flirt with him and make him think you want him, he still might not tell you anything" Maggie said sadly.

"I have to try" Lacey muttered. "And I'm asking that you don't interfere. No matter what you see us doing, please stay out of it."

Maggie looked horrified at the idea. She shook her head, her curls bounced around her face. "This is crazy. I'm not going to let you do this. Cole wouldn't want you to throw yourself at his brother, not even to find him."

Lacey flinched from the harshness of her words. "I'm not going to throw myself at him, Maggie. I'm just going to talk with him. Please understand that I have to do this. I can't take not knowing where Cole is any longer. It's eating me up inside."

Maggie eyes began to water. It hurt to hear Lacey talk like that. She looked away and crossed her arms over her chest. Luke came up behind her and wrapped his arms around her waist and whispered in her ear, "It'll be okay, Maggie. I think Lacey knows what she's doing."

She looked at him and he could see that she was having a really hard time accepting what Lacey was going to do. She didn't think it was right. It took a minute for her to be able to speak. She reached for Lacey's hand and gave it a squeeze. "I hope you know what you're doing. If Jesse did kill Cole, he might not like you playing games with him."

"I'll be fine, Maggie. I promise."

A forced smile crossed Maggie's lips as she nodded. "Okay, just don't get too close to him. I don't want to get sick and puke all over everyone if I see him kissing you or something."

"There will be no kissing" Luke said in a thick voice. Lacey looked at him with raised brows.

"Don't look at me like that, Lacey. I'm agreeing to let you try your plan but I will not sit back and watch him kiss you. I have more respect for Cole than to allow that to happen" Luke said in a tone that sounded more and more like one Cole would use.

Lacey smiled at his protectiveness. She found it cute that he thought he was letting her do something, when the truth was no one could stop her even if they tried. "Alright. Let's get this little charade going."

Maggie let out a deep breath and leaned her head on Luke's shoulder as they led the way to the cookout. The music got louder the closer they got to the village. The soft melodies that filled the air reminded Lacey of the night at the bonfire when she and Cole danced. It was the most romantic moment in her life. She smiled at the memory and tucked it away so she could do the task at hand.

They stepped from the trees into the village area. Lacey was surprised to see that so many people were already there. She still hadn't met everyone in the pack and there were quite a few people she didn't know. She stood at the tree line and looked around at all the people she was now in charge of taking care of. She suddenly felt a little overwhelmed.

"Are you alright?" Maggie asked when she noticed the distracted look on Lacey's face.

"I'm fine" she said with a smile and started toward a large group of females near the tables of food. "Time to get to know my pack" she said to herself.

After talking to a few of the women about the food and music, Lacey left the tables to walk around. She waved at Jeremiah when she saw him looking at her as he took meat from the grill. He looked like something was bothering him but she didn't go over and ask him what. She had her own problems at the moment. She didn't see Jesse anywhere. But she did see someone else that she needed to talk to.

She walked over to a small group of men laughing and talking around a fire. Several of the men immediately tensed up when they saw her. Lacey reached out and placed her hand on the shoulder of a man with his back turned to her. Dallas turned around, his smile vanished when he saw her. He jumped backwards and nearly fell into the fire. "What do you want?" he stuttered and looked around for help.

Seeing him so afraid of her made Lacey feel awful. She looked at him apologetically. "I just wanted to say that I'm sorry. I was out of line yesterday, I shouldn't have attacked you."

Dallas just stared at her. Lacey lifted her hand to brush her hair behind her ear and Dallas flinched, no doubt thinking she was going to hurt him again. Lacey saw the fear in his eyes and lowered her head in shame. "I really am sorry" she said in a rush and walked off. Dallas stared after her for a few minutes then rejoined his friends, not really knowing what to think.

"That was nice of you to apologize to him" Kindal said as she came up beside Lacey. "Hopefully he'll never again do whatever he did to make you mad in the first place."

Lacey stopped walking and looked at Kindal. The smile she wore was so friendly that Lacey felt even worse than she did a few seconds ago. She hadn't spent much time with Kindal since she arrived on the mountain and what little time they had spent together usually ended in an argument.

Lacey hadn't realized until that moment how far she had pushed everyone away. She threw her arms around Kindal's neck and hugged her as memories of their old friendship bombarded her. She blinked several times to force back the tears she felt forming in her eyes. Kindal pulled back and held her at arm's length. "What's wrong?"

"Nothing" Lacey said with a small laugh. "I've just missed you, that's all."

Kindal smiled. "Well, I've been here for almost two weeks now."

"I know" Lacey said with a nod. "I guess I owe you an apology too, huh? I haven't been very nice to you lately and I'm sorry. It's just…things are hard for me right now."

Kindal squeeze her arms gently. "You don't owe me anything. I knew you would make time for me when you were ready."

Lacey pulled her close for another hug. "I don't deserve a friend like you."

Kindal laughed, "Let's find Scotty. I know he's been feeling a little down not being able to talk to you. He misses you too, you know. You're like the little sister he never had."

"Yeah, and he's like the goofy older brother I never had" Lacey said with a smile.

As they walked past the table where Luke and Maggie were sitting, Lacey couldn't help but notice the hateful glare Maggie gave Kindal. Lacey smiled at her and shook her head. She didn't understand why those two were so jealous of each other. They were so much alike that there was really no reason for either of them to be jealous of the other.

"Speak of the devil or should I say clown, and he shall appear" Kindal said teasingly when she saw Scotty walking toward them.

The huge grin on his face caused an ache in Lacey's chest. It reminded her of how close they became at the warehouse in Carol Springs. He really was like a brother to her and she had missed him more than she wanted to admit. "Hey Scotty" she said shyly.

"Hey" he said and looked from Lacey to Kindal, not really sure what else he should say. Lacey hadn't made it easy to talk to her lately and he didn't want to say something that would upset her.

"Well don't just stand there. Why don't you ask Lacey to dance?" Kindal said and nudged Lacey toward him, then winked.

Scotty took the hint that Kindal was trying subtly to give him. Lacey was finally ready to spend some time with them. He smiled and held his hand out to her. "What do you say dance partner? Do you still remember some of the moves I taught you from the last time we danced?"

Lacey rolled her eyes and took his hand. The smile that crossed her lips was the first genuine one she'd worn in a long time. "Please don't remind me. Those moves nearly got your arms ripped off if I remember correctly" she said with a laugh.

Scotty chuckled out loud and led her over to where some of the males were playing as a band, exactly the way they had been at the bonfire. The music they played was fast paced and fun but instead of keeping with the pace of the song, Scotty placed his hands on Lacey's hips and started slow dancing.

Lacey tried not to feel uncomfortable as they danced but having everyone watch them made it nearly impossible. She smiled at Scotty as he led her around in a small circle. "I see you haven't lost any of your dancing skills" she said to make small talk.

Scotty lifted her up in the air and spun her around before setting her feet back on the ground. A cocky smile pulled up the corners of his mouth. "Having a good partner makes all the difference."

Lacey was quiet for a while after that. She laid her head against his chest as she grew more comfortable with him. And before she knew what was happening, she found herself apologizing to him too. "I'm really sorry about the way things have turned out, Scotty."

She could feel him let out a deep breath as he tightened his hold around her. "Me too, Lacey" he sighed, "I'm not even going to try and figure out how things got so screwed up. I don't agree with all the decisions you've made but the important thing is you're okay and that's all that matters. Although, I do have to say I hate that Jesse is hurting the way he is. You're both my friends and it's hard to see what's happened to your relationship, you know."

Lacey lifted her head from his chest and looked at him. "I know and I'm sorry but…"

"No buts okay, let's just enjoy this time together as friends and not talk about any of the craziness that's happened over the last couple of months" Scotty said with a smile that looked out of place. He didn't want to hear about how much she loved Cole again. It made him uncomfortable.

"Alright" Lacey said and laid her head against his chest again. The song came to an end and just as they were about to start dancing to the next one, Jesse tapped Scotty on the shoulder. "Mind if I cut in?" he asked as his eyes locked with Lacey's. An awkward silence fell between them.

CHAPTER TEN

Scotty dropped his hands from Lacey's waist and stepped back. "Thanks for the dance. Maybe we can talk again later" he said and walked over to where Kindal was sitting on the ground, watching them.

Lacey immediately felt the loss of comfort she had enjoyed while being near him. "I'd like that" she said.

Scotty smiled at her then took Kindal's beer out of her hand and finished it off for her. She punched him in the arm.

"Will you dance with me, Lacey?" Jesse asked.

She reluctantly turned her attention to him and forced herself to smile. "Okay"

Jesse eased his arm around her waist and pulled her close to his body. Lacey struggled with herself to keep from tensing up from his touch. She forced her body relax.

"Do you remember the last time we danced?" Jesse asked with a smile.

Lacey looked away at the reminder. She did remember. It was the last night of her human life, before everything got so messed up. Before she learned everything that she now knew. Until she realized that she was in love with Cole, that night had been the best of her entire life. Now it was just another reminder of how wrong she was about Jesse. "It seems like such a long time ago" she said quietly.

"It wasn't that long ago. Just a few months back" Jesse said and tightened his arms around her. He leaned his head near her neck. Lacey was afraid he was going to kiss her. Thankfully, he didn't. Instead he took a deep breath and lifted his head with a satisfied grin on his face. "I could breathe in your scent all day long. It's beautiful. So much stronger now than when you were human."

Lacey looked uncomfortable and not sure how to respond. She could feel heat rushing to her cheeks. "Um…thanks, I guess."

Jesse's eyes lit up with amusement as he chuckled out loud. "Are you blushing?" He rubbed the back of his hand softly over her cheek, "It looks like I still have an effect on you after all, don't I?"

Lacey didn't answer his question. Instead, she smiled and rested her head on his chest like she had done with Scotty. She mentally cussed at herself for not controlling her emotions better. But her moment of weakness had nothing to do with Jesse, not really. It was what he said and the fact that Cole had said the exact same thing to her.

As Jesse led her around, weaving around other dancing couples, Lacey caught sight of Maggie and Luke standing by one of the school cabins. The stressed looks on their faces let her know they were having a hard time keeping to the deal they made with her. But it was the look of total shock on Jeremiah's face that really bothered her.

He wasn't aware of everything she'd found out over the last few days or the fact that she was only pretending to be interested in Jesse. When her eyes met his and he turned and walked away, she felt crushed. She didn't want him to think she was betraying Cole. She closed her eyes and hoped he would understand when he learned the truth.

The song came to an end and Jesse raised his brows in question, "one more?"

Lacey shook her head, "maybe later. Let's just sit and talk for a while." She stepped out of his arms to put some distance between them. He smiled and grabbed her hand, lacing his fingers through hers. Her instincts were to jerk her hand away but she didn't. She needed him to feel comfortable around her.

"Sounds like a good idea. I've been waiting all day to talk with you" Jesse said and led her over to one of the picnic tables closest to the woods, away from everyone else. They sat down across from each other, still holding hands over the table. "I want to start by saying that I'm sorry about last night. I shouldn't have left you in the woods the way I did. But I wasn't prepared to talk about my father and I guess you caught me off guard."

Lacey was quiet for a minute as she thought about the best way to respond. She wanted to jump straight in to asking about Cole but she didn't think that was a good idea. She didn't want Jesse to clam up and not want to talk anymore. "It's alright. I shouldn't have blindsided you the way I did. But now that we're on the subject, can I ask you what happened with your dad?" She squeezed his hand to encourage him.

A dark look crossed his face before he covered it with a smile that didn't reach his eyes. "Well from what you said last night, you already know what happened. I had my father killed."

Lacey was speechless as she stared at him. She hadn't expected him to confess so easily. Hearing it come from his mouth somehow made what he'd done even worse. Maybe it was because she didn't hear even the tiniest bit of remorse in his voice. It took her a moment to be able to speak. "Why?" she asked in a shocked voice. "Why did you do that to your father?"

Jesse released her hand. It was clear he didn't want to have this conversation. "When we first met, you told me about your parents, about how your father abandoned you and your mother wanted nothing to do with you. Well, do you remember what I told you about my mother?"

Lacey nodded, "Yes, you said she killed herself." The sadness she saw in Jesse's eyes after she answered him reminded her of how devastated Cole had looked the night he told her about his father's death.

"Yeah, she did. My mother killed herself because she couldn't stand living the rest of her life as the monster my father turned her into" he sighed, "Your mother was afraid of you, but I think deep down, mine hated me. She hated what Cole and I were just as much as she hated what she was. She never wanted this life, my father forced it on her. But even so, she tried to be a good mother. She always said that she loved me. She took care of me and tucked me into bed every night. But there was always a sad-ness in her eyes that I never understood. My father told me her bouts of depression were because her body didn't completely take to the change and it had affected her mentally. But he swore to me that she would be alright. He kept saying she would get better over time, but she didn't. She got worse."

Jesse lowered his head and shook it from side to side, "don't you see? It was his fault. She's dead because he was so selfish that he didn't care about whether or not she wanted to be changed, he did it because it was what he wanted."

"So instead of losing just one parent you decided to get rid of the other one as well" Lacey said in a low voice and looked at him sympathetically. "Tell me, Jesse, did having your father killed make anything better? Did it bring your mom back? Did it take away your pain?" She waited for him to answer.

He stared at her for a minute before looking away and shaking his head. "No" he said sadly, "It didn't. But I'm not sorry for what I did. Over the years I've tried to be but I'm just not. I loved my mother so much and I hated my father for what he did to her."

"Don't you understand that if he hadn't changed her you wouldn't be here right now? You never would have been born."

Jesse nodded. "I know. But at least she would still be alive, living a nice, normal, human life somewhere."

Lacey stood up and went around the table and sat down beside him. She placed her hand on his arm as she spoke. "You can't think like that. No one knows what kind of life she would have had if she hadn't met your father. What happened to her was a terrible tragedy but I don't think your father meant for it to happen. He must have loved her very much to have chosen her as his mate. That has to mean something to you."

Jesse lifted his hand and rubbed it along her cheek. "I wish it did, but it doesn't. Loving someone doesn't give you the right to take away their humanity." He let his hand drop, "just look at us. I love you more than anything in the world but when you came to me that night at the warehouse and asked me about changing humans, I think deep down I knew you were talking about yourself and I still said no. I regret that decision now. But my father could have walked away from my mother, she wasn't in the same position you were in, she wasn't about to die when he changed her."

Not knowing what else to say, Lacey remained silent. Neither of them said another word for several minutes. Finally Jesse broke the silence. He eased his arm around Lacey's shoulder, "how about another dance?" he asked to change the subject.

Lacey looked over at everyone dancing. Kindal and Scotty were mixed in with the crowd making a show of themselves as they danced wildly with each other. Dean and Joel were having fun with a group of girls. And Maggie and Luke were holding each other close as they moved around in a tight circle, slow dancing to a fast paced song. Lacey smiled at them but they didn't notice. They only had eyes for each other. She turned her attention back to Jesse. "Next song, okay."

Jesse smiled and pulled her closer to him. Since things were going so well, she decided to take a chance and ask him about Cole. "Can I ask you something?"

"I guess so" he said and snuck a kiss to the side of her head.

Lacey shyly brushed her hand down her hair to straighten it and push him back a little. "Last night when you said that Cole got what he deserved. What did you mean by that?"

Jesse lifted his arm from her shoulder and shook his head in an annoyed gesture. "Can't we have just one day without talking about him?" His jaw clenched as he ground his teeth together. "I mean damn, when are you going to accept that he's gone? He's never coming back so there's no point in talking about him anymore. He's dead, Lacey. Get over it" he said with an edge to his voice. The comfortable air that had been present between them just moments ago was now gone.

Lacey could tell he was getting mad and that made her own temper rise. He was avoiding her question and she was losing her patience with trying to play nice. She stood up from the table and narrowed her eyes at him. "What did you mean by what you said about Cole?" she asked again, her voice tight with the strain of trying to keep herself calm.

Jesse jumped up and stood in front of her. "I meant I'm not sorry that he's dead. I hated him just like he hated me. He fell off the cliff. He died. End of story. To me, he got what he deserved for all the lives he took. Any more questions?" he asked coldly. But before Lacey could respond, he grabbed her by the shoulders and pulled her close, crushing his mouth to hers.

The kiss was rough and unwanted. And it really pissed her off. She raised her hands to his chest and tried to push him back but he tightened his hold on her shoulders and forced her mouth open with his tongue. Her anger triggered her wolf and she was clawing to get free. Lacey forced her back and renewed her struggle. She lifted the hold on her power just enough to force Jesse away.

His feet skidded across the ground as he was forced backwards several feet.

"Don't ever do that again!" Lacey yelled and wiped her hand across her mouth. She was staring angrily at him and didn't notice that their little exchange had garnered an audience until it was too late.

Out of nowhere, Luke tackled Jesse to the ground and started punching him in the face. Jeremiah and several other males ran to break up the fight. Within seconds, Maggie was by Lacey's side. "Are you alright?" she asked in a worried tone.

Lacey nodded and watched as Jeremiah pulled Luke off of Jesse. "I warned you!" Luke growled and tried to break free of his father's hold. "I told you to stay the hell away from her."

Jesse lifted his upper lip in a snarl and took a step toward him. Scotty quickly stood between them and put his hand on Jesse's chest and pushed him back. "You can't do this, Jesse. Not now. We're majorly outnumbered and this is his territory. Just calm down, buddy" he whispered near his ear.

Jesse pushed Scotty away and pointed his finger at Luke, "I don't take orders from you, kid. I suggest you keep your distance from me because your daddy might not be there to break us up next time."

"I hope he won't be" Luke growled back. He jerked his arms from Jeremiah's grip and walked over to Maggie and Lacey.

With the way Jesse was looking at Lacey with longing, Scotty knew that he wanted to go over there too. So to avoid another fight, he put his hand on Jesse's back and said, "how about a beer?" And urged him toward the cooler by the food tables.

Jesse was hesitant at first but when Lacey turned her back to him to talk to her friends, he allowed Scotty to lead him away.

"You really know how to get some attention, don't you?" Scotty said teasingly. But Jesse didn't think it was funny. He narrowed his eyes at him as a small growl escaped his throat. Scotty lost his smile, "sorry, bad joke" he said quickly and grabbed two beers from the cooler. They saw Kindal sitting by herself and made their way over to her.

"What the hell was that all about?" Luke asked Lacey as she sat down at the table.

"I don't know. We were talking and then he just grabbed me."

Maggie noticed blood on Lacey's lip and she balled her hands into fists. Surprised by her action, Luke looked at Maggie. The anger he saw on her face was uncharacteristic for her. "What's wrong?" he asked.

"She's bleeding" Maggie said and pointed to Lacey's lip. "That bastard bit her!"

Both Lacey and Luke's eyes grew wide as they stared at Maggie. It was the first swear word either of them had ever heard her say and it shocked them. She raised her brows and stared back at them, daring them to say something about her choice of words. "What?"

Lacey couldn't help but laugh. She shook her head and touched her finger to her lip then wiped the small dab of blood on her jeans. "He didn't bite me. It was just a really rough kiss."

"He better not do that again" Luke said before sitting down at the table and pulling Maggie down onto his lap.

A few minutes later, Lacey saw Jeremiah coming toward their table. Considering the way he looked at her earlier – like he thought she was betraying Cole, she was too embarrassed to stay and talk to him. She jumped up from the table, "Um, I think I've mingled with the pack enough for one day. I'm going to go. I'll see you guys later" she said, in a hurry to leave before Jeremiah reached them.

"Wait. Did you get any information from Jesse? Are you going to start searching again? If you are, we'll go with you" Maggie said.

"Um, no…Jesse didn't say anything useful and I'm just going for a walk right now. I'll meet up with you later and we'll pick up the search where we left off. Okay?"

Maggie nodded and Lacey quickly headed into the woods.

Luke knew the second he saw the worried look on his father's face as he approached the table that something was wrong.

"Have you seen your mother? I still can't find her" Jeremiah said in a thick voice.

"Sorry dad, I haven't seen her."

Jeremiah's body stiffened. "Something is not right around here. I just got word that a couple of strange scents have been detected in the woods. It looks like we have some visitors on the mountain. Where did Lacey go?"

"She went for a walk" Maggie answered.

"Let me know the second she gets back. We need to decide what to do about the newcomers. I haven't caught their scent yet but several others who live closer to the base of the mountain have. It's just a matter of time before our guest make their way here. And until we know who they are and what they want we need to keep our guard up."

CHAPTER ELEVEN

Lacey wondered through the woods with no clear destination in mind. She just needed to get away from everyone for a little while. So when she realized where she had gone, she was surprised. She stopped in front of the run-downed cabin as a flood of emotions rushed into her.

She had only been to Cole's childhood home once and that was the night she lost him. So much had happened that night and she hadn't given any thought to the cabin or the promise she'd made to Cole, until that moment. She brought her hand up to her mouth as warm tears slid down her cheeks.

The cabin was supposed to be their new home. It was where they were going to live after they were mated. Seeing it now and knowing that their plan was never going to happen devastated her. She fell to the ground on her knees as a wave of despair crushed her.

She was so tired, both emotionally and physically. After almost two weeks of nonstop searching and battling with herself to keep hope that Cole was still alive despite all the evidence to the contrary, she was exhausted. Whether he was alive or dead, whether Jesse killed him or someone else did - she just didn't know what to believe anymore. Her mind was a confused mess.

She reached into the front pocket of her jeans and pulled out the wad of Cole's hair that she found in the woods. She lifted it to her nose and inhaled the little scent that still remained on it. Instead of comforting her the way she had hoped it would, the reminder of his scent sent her into a round of uncontrollable sobs.

She closed her fist around the hair and held it to her chest as her whole body shook. She was so lost in her breakdown that she didn't notice she was no longer alone until someone put their hand on her shoulder.

Startled, she jumped to her feet and spun around to face whoever was behind her. When she saw Dean's freckled face staring at her wide-eyed like he was afraid she was going to attack him, she closed her eyes and let out a deep calming breath. After a few seconds, she opened her eyes and turned back toward the cabin. She stared at it as she talked, "what are you doing here? Did you follow me?" She brushed her hand roughly across her cheek to wipe away her tears.

"Uh...no, I didn't. I was on my way home and I caught your scent. I wanted to see if you were okay. I saw what happened in the village" Dean said shyly.

Lacey could hear the apprehension in his voice and she hated knowing that he was afraid of her just like everyone else. They had talked a couple times over the last few weeks and she considered him a friend. She didn't feel like she needed to put her guard up around him.

She looked at Dean - her eyes red and swollen - and forced a small smile to her face. "I'm okay" she said and pointed to the cabin, "Did you know this was supposed to be my new home. Cole and I were going to fix it up and move in." A thick lump formed in her throat. "Now I guess I'm technically homeless. Again"

"Yeah, I heard about what happened to your cabin last night. So I guess you are kind of homeless, huh? Wait...what do you mean again?" Dean asked curiously.

"It's a long story and not one I want to talk about right now" Lacey said quickly to put an end to any questions he might want to ask about her life before she came to the mountain.

Dean was quiet for a few seconds as he watched Lacey stare at the cabin. "This place means a lot to you, doesn't it?"

She looked at him with sad eyes and nodded. "This is where Cole grew up. It's a part of who he is…or was. And until I came here today, I didn't realize how badly I need some kind of connection to him."

Dean walked past her and over to the cabin. He surveyed it from the outside then stepped onto the porch and opened the door and looked inside. He looked at Lacey with a big smile on his face. "I can fix it up for you. And it wouldn't take very long either. I know Joel has a whole shed full of logs and lumber that were left over from when he built his cabin last year. And I have more than enough paint for the walls at my place. I'd say in about two days I can have this place looking good as new if you want me to."

"You would do that for me?" Lacey asked, surprised by his offer.

"Of course. You're the alpha female and my friend" he said shyly. "Besides, I'm pretty sure Cole would have wanted you to stay here."

Lacey hurried up the steps of the porch and threw her arms around Dean's neck and hugged him. "Thank you. Thank you so much. I'd love for you to fix the place up for me."

Dean cautiously hugged her back. It was the first physical contact they'd shared and he was kind of nervous, especially since he knew that touching her could send him flying into a tree or something. He timidly patted her on the back before stepping away from her. "You're welcome. I can get started now if you want me to. I'll just need to go find Joel and a couple of my friends first."

"Okay. That sounds good. Thank you again, Dean. I can't tell you how much this means to me."

He smiled. "Just do me a favor okay, wait until we're done before you come back to see it. I want it to be a surprise."

"I can do that. I'm probably going to be staying at Maggie's, so whenever you're done just let me know" Lacey said and started walking off into the woods.

"Lacey" Dean called after her. She looked over her shoulder at him. "I'm really sorry about what happened to Cole."

"Me too" Lacey said to herself as she stepped into the woods. Once out of Dean's sight, she took her clothes off and stuffed them in a hole at the trunk of a tree before dropping to the ground on all fours and letting her wolf take over.

She suddenly had an urge to run and needed more speed than her human form could allow. She took off through the woods hoping to outrun the pain filling her heart at the thought that it might truly be time to let Cole go after all.

*****

Cole groaned as he slowly regained consciousness. His body was so weak that it had grown numb to the pain that had caused him to pass out. He looked up through heavy lids to see that the chains around his wrists had dug all the way into his flesh and were touching his bone. He closed his eyes as helplessness consumed him.

"Welcome back" Mira said in an uncharacteristically sincere voice. "I was beginning to get worried that I was going to have to find a way out of here all by myself."

Cole let out a tired sigh, "We aren't getting out of here, Mira. I don't know about you, but I know that I'm going to die here."

"Don't say that!" Mira growled in frustration and fear. "Don't you dare give up! You're closer to being rescued now than you've ever been. Jeremiah has to be looking for me by now. He's going to find us."

Cole could hear a bit of hysteria in her voice. "He might get here in time to save you, but not me. I'm too weak. I haven't eaten in weeks. My body isn't able to heal itself anymore. I've lost a lot of blood and I think infection is growing in my wounds. I'm dying, Mira" he said in a ragged breath.

"No, you're not. Damn it!" she yelled. "You have to keep fighting. You have to fight for Lacey."

"I can't fight anymore. I don't have the strength to."

Mira began to panic. "Then you have to find the strength to fight. Think of Lacey and how hard she's been searching for you."

Mira had never been a fan of Cole's but at the moment she felt a connection to him and she didn't want to lose it. Whether it was because they were both trapped with no way of getting back to their loved ones or because she was actually starting to like him as a friend, she didn't know or care. She just didn't want to be left alone.

Cole didn't say anything. Mira cocked her head to the side and focused on trying to hear his heartbeat. She could hear it, but it was faint. She called out to him but he still didn't respond. Her panic was quickly turning into anger. "Damn you, Cole! Answer me!" She knew that she had to keep him talking.

"What?" Cole's voice was barely a whisper.

Mira let out a relieved breath. "You need to stay with me now. Talk. Don't close your eyes, okay?"

"What do you want to talk about?"

Mira racked her brain for something to say but she came up empty. "Um, I don't know. Just ask me something. Anything."

Cole was once again silent as he thought. "Alright. Earlier you admitted that you didn't like Lacey because you knew she was stronger than you. So what's your excuse for the way you've mistreated Maggie all these years. And don't say it's because she's stronger than you too, because we both know that's not true." His words were weak and drawn out.

Mira closed her eyes and shook her head. Of all the things he could have asked her, she hated that her relationship with Maggie or lack of one, was what he wanted to talk about. But at the moment, she needed to keep him talking no matter how uncomfortable she was with their discussion.

"Maggie is a lot stronger than you think, Cole. But you're right, her strength isn't in the way she fights or stands up for herself. It's in the way she loves and cares for others, which is something I'm just not good at. No matter what I've done to try and separate her and Luke, she doesn't back down. Any of the other females in the pack would have long ago given up on being with Luke just to avoid having to deal with me. But not Maggie. She really loves him and I guess I'm afraid that Luke loves her more than me."

"So all of these years of tormenting Maggie were because you're jealous? That's an emotion I never imagined you capable of feeling. You're just full of surprises, aren't you?"

Mira ignored his jab and started talking about Jeremiah. Cole listened as she went on and on about how he was probably on his way to find them at that very moment. When she finally stopped talking to take a breath, Cole took the opportunity to speak. "Mira, will you do me a favor?"

"I don't know. The last time I did a favor for someone I ended up here with you" she said dryly.

"Please" he pleaded in a low voice.

"Fine. What do you want me to do?" she said in a gruff tone.

Cole was quiet as he thought about what he wanted to say. When he finally spoke, Mira could hear the way he was struggling to breathe. "I want you to tell Lacey that I love her. Tell her she is the best thing that ever happened to me. And tell her I'm sorry for not being strong enough to find my way back to her."

Mira's heart clenched at the sadness of his words. She shook her head as a thick lump formed in her throat. "No. No, I won't do that. You can tell her yourself. It won't be long now before someone finds us. You just need to hold on a little longer."

Cole didn't respond. There was no sense in arguing with Mira when he knew he only had a little time left. He didn't want to spend it fighting with her. He closed his eyes and thought about Lacey. He desperately wanted her face to be the last thing he saw before he died.

*****

Lacey's run through the woods had calmed her down and now that she had retrieved her clothes and changed back to her human form, she made her way back to the village. The scene before her as she stepped from the woods was much different than it had been before she ran off.

The band was no longer playing music and instead of dancing and eating, everyone was huddled in a tight circle around one of the tables. Lacey could hear Jeremiah's voice as he spoke to the crowd. She had barely taken two steps before everyone turned around to look at her. She sighed deeply. She still wasn't completely used to the fact that her scent always announced her arrival. It made it difficult to observe things from afar.

Maggie broke from the group and ran toward her with a worried look on her face. "Thank heavens, you're back. We were just about to go looking for you."

Lacey raised her brows in confusion. "Why? What's going on?"

"We have strangers on the mountain. Their scents were detected earlier near the base of the mountain but now they're getting closer" Maggie said in a rush and wrapped her arm around Lacey's shoulder and led her over to the center of the group to stand beside Jeremiah and Luke.

Lacey looked at Jeremiah. "Are they human or like us?"

"They are our kind" he said and pierced her with a serious look.

Lacey could tell that there was more to the hard expression on his face than just a few uninvited wolves. And when she noticed the stressed looks on Maggie and Luke, she knew she was right. "What aren't you telling me?" she asked in a cautious tone.

"Dad and I went scouting after you left for your walk" Luke said, "we caught the scent of the newcomers and we recognized one of them."

"Well, who is it?" Lacey asked without patience.

"It's Zack" a voice from the crowd said.

Lacey searched through the faces staring at her until her eyes landed on Jesse. He was standing with his arms crossed over his chest with Kindal and Scotty flanking him.

Lacey stood silent and stared at him. She knew that there was a possibility Zack was still alive. Although, she had hoped he was dead.

Maggie took her silence as fear and grabbed her hand. "Don't worry, Lacey. We don't know what he wants but we won't let him anywhere near you, I promise."

"You got that right" Jesse growled as he approached Lacey. He stopped in front of her and lifted his hand to touch her face. Maggie surprised everyone by growling at him. Lacey gave her hand a gentle squeeze to calm her down.

"Your friend is right" Jesse said and dropped his hand back to his side, "Zack isn't going to come near you. I'll kill him before he gets within a hundred feet of you. I should have taken care of him a long time ago."

Lacey looked around at her friends, confusion clear on her face. "Why do you all think he's coming for me? I haven't done anything to him."

Scotty stepped up beside Jesse. "Well, if you ask me, it could be one of two reasons. Number one: Zack and Sasha were lovers. He might want revenge for you killing her. And number two: I hate to say this but he might want you because of your powers. He might think he can use you somehow."

"I agree with Scotty" Kindal said as she joined the discussion.

Lacey shook her head in disagreement. "I don't know. I guess it's possible but I don't think Zack and Sasha were really that close. I mean if they were, why did Sasha come here to get Cole back? And as far as my powers, Zack knows he's no match against me. He can't even get close enough to hurt me unless I allow him to."

Everyone was quiet as they considered what she said. They all knew she had a point about her powers. But no one really knew how close Zack and Sasha were.

"Maybe him being here doesn't have anything to do with Lacey" Jeremiah said in a thick voice. Everyone turned their attention to him.

"He's right" Luke said as he looked at his father. Their eyes met and they knew that they were both thinking the same thing. "Mom is still missing. Maybe Zack and his friends have her" Luke said in a strained voice.

"Whoa! What? Mira still hasn't come home?" Lacey asked with a bit of panic in her voice.

Jesse's body tensed when he heard Mira's name, but no one noticed. Not wanting to take the chance that his physical reactions would give him away, he inched further away from Lacey to blend in with the crowd.

"No" Maggie said sadly and gave Luke a sympathetic look.

"Then we have to start looking for her right now!" Lacey said with authority. She jumped right into yelling orders at everyone. She broke the crowd up into several small groups to send out in search parties. "All of you stay within hearing distance of your group members for safety. We don't know what's going on right now and I don't want Zack and his friends to be able to pick you off one by one. If you find Mira or detect her scent anywhere, send someone to find me immediately."

The seventy or so people in front of her all nodded before quickly dispersing into the woods, some in human form, others as wolves. Lacey then looked at the few people still standing near her. She noticed Jesse walking toward the trees, behind one of the search groups and called out to him. He stopped and looked at her. "We could use your help in another group" she said and waited for him to respond.

Jesse looked at her for a second before glancing toward the trees. He hadn't planned on helping the search group he was following. He was just looking for a way to get away from everyone so he could hurry to the cabin and dispose of Cole and Mira before someone found them.

"Jesse" Lacey called out to him again, her voice void of patience.

Reluctantly, he turned around and started toward her. Every fiber in his body tensed as he fought the urge to dart into the woods. He approached the group standing with Lacey.

Scotty put his hand on Jesse's shoulder and whispered, "We need the best with us, buddy."

Jesse shot him a look that made him quickly remove his hand. Scotty backed away but kept his eyes on Jesse. He cocked his head to the side and tried to figure out what was going on with him. He could feel the tension in his body when he touched him and he could sense the fear building inside him. "Everything alright?" Scotty asked.

Jesse gave him a hard look before turning his head to look at Lacey. "Everything's fine" he snapped.

Scotty looked at him skeptically before moving to stand beside Kindal a few feet away. He couldn't help but think something wasn't right with Jesse.

CHAPTER TWELVE

"Alright, Jeremiah, Jesse and Kindal, you three should search together. And Luke, Maggie and Scotty, you guys can be another group. Stick together and…" Lacey was interrupted by Jeremiah and then by Maggie.

"I don't need to search with anyone. Mira is my mate. I will search for her on my own."

"What about you?" Maggie asked Lacey. "Who are you going to search with?"

Lacey narrowed her eyes at Jeremiah. "I know she's your mate, which is exactly why you don't need to search on your own. You're emotionally distressed right now. You might overlook something that can put you and Mira in danger."

Jeremiah opened his mouth to argue but Lacey stopped him by speaking first, "I hate to pull this card with you, Jeremiah, but I am in charge here. You said that I needed to take my position more seriously, well that's what I'm doing. Now take Jesse and Kindal and go find Mira." She paused and looked at Maggie, "and as for your question…I'll catch up with you and Luke in a little while. I have something I need to do first."

Maggie accepted her answer. "Okay"

Jeremiah was silent for a second then he glanced in Jesse and Kindal's direction, "let's go" he said roughly before storming off toward the woods.

Jesse nodded at Kindal and she fell into step behind Jeremiah. After looking at Lacey once more, Jesse grudgingly followed after them. But he had no intention of staying with his group. As soon as he got a chance, he planned on ditching them so that he could make sure no one ever found Mira or Cole, at least not alive. And now that Zack was on the mountain, he had the perfect fall guy. If anyone did find the bodies, they would assume Zack and his pack were responsible.

Maggie and Luke looked at Scotty as he started stripping. He smiled at them and dropped his shirt to the ground then shifted into his wolf form. Lacey walked off and headed toward the trees alone.

"Where exactly are you going?" Maggie yelled after her.

Lacey glanced over her shoulder and smiled thinly, "don't worry about me, Maggie. I'll be fine" she said and stepped into the woods with her destination clear in mind.

She was confident that her pack would search every inch of the mountain for Mira, and even for Zack and his pack. That is unless they were hiding in the one part of the mountain that was forbidden to her pack members.

She took off at a dead run through the woods hoping that she would be the one to find Zack and his men before they had the chance to hurt anyone. She could feel her wolf struggling to get free. The adrenaline that coursed through her body brought the wolf closer to the surface, but Lacey forced her back. She needed to be in human form in case she found Mira and she was injured.

Denying her wolf freed a path for her powers to get out. Lacey tightened her mental hold on them, but as she pushed herself to run faster, she lost concentration and her hold slipped a bit. From the corner of her eyes, she saw the trees swaying from side to side even though there was no wind. She clamped down on her powers and forced them to the back of her mind.

After nearly half an hour of nonstop running, Lacey came to the fence that separated the two parts of the mountain. Without wasting any time, she quickly slipped through the hole and started running again, hoping to catch someone's scent. Whether it be Mira's or one of Zack's men.

Lacey surveyed everything she passed as she ran. Nothing seemed out of place and there were no strange scents in the air, at least not until she got a good mile or so away from the fence. She skidded to an abrupt stop when a familiar scent hit her nose. It was barely detectable but Mira's scent was in the air. And so was someone else's.

Lacey stood still and inhaled deeply, hoping to get a better whiff of the scent to prove the assumption in her mind was wrong. But all it did was confirm what she already knew. Jesse's scent was also in the air. But it wasn't a fresh scent, it was almost completely gone. Just like Mira's. It was as if they had been there together at an earlier time, but that didn't make sense. Why would they have been there together?

All of a sudden the conversation Lacey had with Mira the day before popped into her head. She had asked Mira to follow Jesse. And considering both of their scents were in a place they shouldn't be, Mira must have done what was asked of her. A string of questions formed in Lacey's mind but she didn't have time to think about them.

She lifted her nose in the air and tried to track Mira's scent. She followed the faint scent for several hundred feet. When it started getting stronger, Lacey picked up her pace. The further she went, the stronger the scent became. Relief that she was about to find Mira washed over her and she started running. But when another scent became detectable, she tripped and nearly fell on her face.

She scrambled to her feet as her heart pounded in her chest. With her breathing labored, her eyes frantically searched the woods around her for the source of the scent that was about to send her back to her knees. It was a scent she knew well. One she never thought she would smell again. "Cole" she whispered in disbelief. It seemed so surreal that after all the time she had spent searching for him, she was finally close enough to smell him.

She quickly pulled herself together and started running again, this time tracking both Mira and Cole's scents. In the back of her mind, she tried to put everything together as she ran. When the scents led her to a huge mound of bushes and broken tree limbs, her heart fell to her feet. An image of Cole's body laying hidden somewhere in the bushes flashed in her mind and caused a pain-filled gasp to escape her lips. "No"

Needing to know that the picture her mind conjured up wasn't real, she stepped closer to the bushes. Almost immediately she heard something that shouldn't have been there. Heartbeats. Lacey started pulling at the bushes until her hands touched wood. "What the hell?" she said to herself. All of a sudden, she heard movement from the other side of the wood. "Hello?" she called out.

Mira's quick respond shocked her. "Lacey? Is that you?" her voice was muffled through what Lacey now knew was the wall of a cabin.

"Yes, it's me" Lacey said and quickly pulled away the rest of the bushes until she saw the door. Without hesitation, she pushed the door open and rushed inside the small cabin.

"In here!" Mira yelled, "We're in here" she said frantically.

Lacey didn't need Mira to tell her where they were, she knew instantly. Their scents were so strong inside the cabin. She made her way to the back. She was shaking by the time she reached the open doorway of the back room. She was finally going to see Cole again. Her emotions were such a jumbled mess that the hold she kept on her powers was no longer in place. The entire cabin started vibrating. She slowly stepped toward the room that Cole's scent was spilling out of. What she saw when she looked inside the room made her heart stop beating.

Mira was chained at the foot of an old metal bed and Cole was suspended in the air with his hands and legs chained to both ends of the bed frame. And he wasn't moving.

Lacey rushed into the room, passed Mira and looked down at Cole. A small burst of energy left her body and instantly all his chains snapped. Instead of his body hitting the floor hard like it should have, it gently moved through the air and settled easily on the floor by Lacey's feet.

She knelt down beside him as tears flowed from her eyes. Mira was yelling at her to free her too, but Lacey didn't as much as look her way. However, with one swing of her hand, Mira's chains broke.

Lacey lifted Cole's head onto her lap and rubbed her hand over his face. He looked as if he had lost twenty pounds or more. His skin was extremely dry and pale. His eyes were sunk in, with dark bags under them. The pain that filled her at seeing him look so close to death was overwhelming. She glanced down at his hands and a sob escaped her throat when she saw the damage done to his wrists. "Oh Cole, what have they done to you?" she whispered sadly.

He slowly opened his eyes halfway. A small smile spread across his dry, cracked lips. "Why did you wake me, Mira? I was having the most amazing dream. I heard her voice. I heard Lacey" he said in a dazed, rough whisper.

Mira knelt down on the other side of him and rested her hand on his shoulder. "You weren't dreaming, Cole. Lacey is here. She's come to help you."

Cole opened his eyes all the way and stared up at Lacey as she spoke to him again. He blinked several times to get better focus.

"She's right, Cole. I came to take you home" Lacey said as warm tears rolled down her cheek and landed on his face. He lifted his hand and rested it on her cheek as his own eyes began to water. "Is it really you?"

Unable to speak through the thick lump in her throat, Lacey brought his hand to her lips and kissed the back of it. She swallowed hard and nodded. "It's really me, Cole. I'm going to take you to get some help."

He gave her hand a weak squeeze and shook his head. "I love you so much, Lacey. But it's too late. I'm dying" he said solemnly.

Lacey jerked backwards, shaking her head. "No. No, don't say that. I won't let you die. Do you hear me?"

Before Cole could respond, he lost consciousness again.

"Cole? Cole!" Lacey screamed his name as panic overtook her. Mira grabbed her by the arm and squeezed. "Lacey, calm down. He's been doing this for the last couple of hours. He'll wake up again soon, okay. His body is very weak and if we don't get him to the doctor now, he will die." She paused, "I don't know how we are going to do it but we have to get him out of here before Jesse comes back."

A dark look crossed Lacey's face. "Jesse? He did this to Cole?"

"Yes" Mira said in a rush and started moving around the cabin, searching for something. When she felt the surge of power building up in Lacey, she immediately went to her. She knew she had to calm her down before things got out of control. "Lacey, I know you're mad, judging from the power I feel radiating off of you, you're really mad. But we can't afford for you to lose it right now, okay. You have to think of Cole, he needs help."

Lacey's nostrils flared and she ground her teeth together. She knew that there was a strong possibility Jesse was involved with Cole's disappearance, but once she learned Zack was on the mountain she had hoped he was the one responsible for keeping Cole from her.

Hearing Mira confirm that it was Jesse afterall, filled her with so much rage that she couldn't contain it. All of the hair on her body stood on ends and the air sizzled around her. Knowing that Jesse had betrayed her, and lied to her face again and again, was too much. She wanted to lash out at something. She needed a release to get rid of some of the turmoil boiling inside her that was preventing her from thinking straight.

She looked down at Cole as her powers forced their way out. A scream built in her throat. All of a sudden, the cabin exploded outward around them. The ceiling came crashing down, but Lacey used her powers to divert the debris from landing on them. Mira fell to the ground in the fetal position with her hands covering her head.

When Lacey stopped screaming and light from the sun shined on her face, Mira opened her eyes to see that the entire cabin was gone. Nothing was left but the floor beneath them. She glared at Lacey as she sagged forward and let out a deep breath. "You feel better now?" she asked sarcastically.

Lacey wouldn't look at her. She kept her eyes on Cole and shook her head. "No, I don't. But I will once we get him out of here."

"How are we going to do that? He can't walk and he's too heavy for us to carry him all the way to the village" Mira said.

As Lacey stared at Cole, a thought formed in her mind. She didn't know if it would work but she was willing to do whatever it took to save him. She opened herself up to her power and let it flow through her unchallenged. Using her mind, she lifted Cole from the floor and slowly sent him floating through the air.

Mira watched wide-eyed as Lacey walked beside him. "Can you do this" she pointed to Cole suspended in the air, "all the way to the village?"

"I don't know" Lacey said and increased the speed in which Cole flew through the air. She glanced at Mira, "Let's go. This isn't as easy as it looks. I can already feel the strain using my powers is taking on me."

Lacey and Mira had to run to keep up with Cole as he flew through the air. Lacey had to pay close attention and concentrate hard to keep him from slamming into trees in their path. By the time they got to the fence, she was breathing heavily. The strain of using her powers steadily and the strength it took to keep Cole levitated was quickly draining her.

After using a sharp bust of power to lift Cole over the fence, Lacey went through the hole then sagged against the fence. Cole's body lowered to the ground as she struggled to fight against the drain of energy.

"Are you alright?" Mira asked when she noticed the tired look on Lacey's face.

"I just need a minute. I've never used my powers like this before" she gasped out between breaths. After a couple of seconds, she took a deep breath and Cole slowly lifted into the air again, but not nearly as high as before. Lacey looked at him and shook her head.

"What's wrong?" Mira asked.

"We're not going to make it to the village. My powers are weakening. And using them is draining me of energy. We need help. You go on ahead. Find Jeremiah, he's out here somewhere looking for you."

Mira look at Lacey and then at Cole. She didn't want to leave them alone but she knew Lacey was right, they couldn't get Cole all the way to the village on their own. "What if Jesse finds you? There is no telling what he might do."

"Let me worry about Jesse. You just go get us some help. We'll be right behind you. I just can't go as fast as you." The strain in her voice was more noticeable.

"Alright" Mira said and quickly shifted into her wolf form and took off through the woods.

Lacey pushed away from the fence and concentrated on keeping Cole elevated in the air. She used everything she had left to send him floating in front of her as she slowly jogged through the woods. She only made it a couple hundred feet before the strain on her mind became too much and she stumbled and fell to the ground. Cole crashed beside her.

Lacey was almost completely drained of energy and was fighting a round of dizziness that was threatening to send her into unconsciousness. "Lacey" Cole's weak voice made her open her tired eyes. She looked over at him, sprawled out on the ground beside her.

His eyes were only half open, but she could see the green that she loved so much. She just stared at him, unwilling to break the eye contact they had. Neither of them said a word as they stared at each other. There was no need for talking. A million different things were said with the way they looked at each other.

It wasn't until an alarming scent filled the air around them that Lacey tore her eyes away from Cole and forced herself to sit up. She scanned the woods looking for the threat she knew was near. Zack was close by and from the number of different scents she smelled, he wasn't alone.

Lacey scrambled to her feet as her natural instincts to survive and to keep the man she loved safe kicked in. Zack's scent was getting closer. She looked down at Cole, her heart filled with so much love and fear that it felt as if it was going to explode.

"Just go. Leave me and run" Cole said when he finally caught the scents in the air. He closed his eyes and blamed himself for the weak state Lacey was now in. "You're too weak to fight him. Run."

"No" Lacey said with a shake of her head. "I'm not leaving you, so shut up and let me think" she said in a determined voice. After a few minutes, she kissed him gently on the lips and did the best she could not to let the tears she felt building in her eyes slip free. It broke her heart to know that she was going to have to leave him, even though she didn't want to. "I'll be back, I promise. Stay quiet."

Before Cole could respond, she stepped away from him, putting at least thirty feet between them. She closed her eyes and summoned all the power she had left to the surface. It wasn't much but it was enough to do what she needed to do.

She sent the power out in short, strong burst in several different directions. Loud cracking and snapping sounds filled the air as all the trees around Cole fell to the ground, cocooning him, but not touching him. Hiding him was the best Lacey could do to protect him. When she was certain that he was well hidden, she stepped close to the pile of trees and knowing that Cole could still hear her, she whispered, "I love you" before walking away to distract Zack and his men.

They were so close now that she knew they had already caught her scent and Cole's. And it was up to her now to lead them away. She started jogging away from Cole. Within a matter of minutes, she could hear others moving through the woods around her. She picked up her pace but even so, it was barely a run. She was too weak to move faster.

From the corner of her eye, she caught a glimpse of a dark brown wolf. Seconds later, she saw several more wolves on her right and left as they ran through the woods trying to catch up with her. She knew they weren't her pack members and pushed herself as hard as she could. But in her weakened state she was no match for the wolves. The burning in her chest as she struggled to breathe and the heaviness of her legs proved too much. She collapsed on the ground and waited for the inevitable. They were going to catch her, but at least Cole was safe.

CHAPTER THIRTEEN

Jeremiah kept his nose to the ground and sniffed through the leaves hoping to catch a whiff of Mira's scent. But once again, there was nothing. Disappointed, he looked over his shoulder at Jesse and Kindal, who were also in their wolf forms. He growled to let them know he was moving on to another location.

Kindal followed him but Jesse lagged behind, staying several feet back. He was looking for an opportunity to get away without looking suspicious. But Jeremiah was more observant than Jesse gave him credit for. Just as he was about to make a run for it, Jeremiah turned around and ran past Kindal and stopped in front of Jesse. He growled at him then stood on his hind legs and shifted into his human form. "What the hell are you up to, Jesse?"

Jesse quickly shifted as well. "What are you talking about?" he said defensively. "I'm out here trying to help you find your mate since you can't seem to keep up with her."

Jeremiah narrowed his eyes at him. "Don't give me that shit. You're up to something and I know it. Do you really think I can't feel the tension and nervousness coming off of you? I can smell the fear on you, you're afraid of something. What is it? What are you so afraid of, Jesse?"

Kindal quickly shifted and tried to wedge herself between them. "Come on guys, don't do this. Calm down. Both of you." No one listened to her.

"I'm not afraid of a damn thing" Jesse growled.

Jeremiah opened his mouth to say something back but then he snapped it shut. He lifted his nose in the air and took a deep breath. The scent that was coming his way made his eyes light up. He pushed past Kindal and Jesse and scanned the woods behind them. It didn't take long for him to find what he was looking for. He let out a deep breath when he saw Mira running toward him in her wolf form.

Jesse's eyes grew wide when he saw her. He didn't know how she had escaped but he knew he was about to be busted. His heart hammered in his chest as fear settled within him. Taking advantage of Jeremiah being distracted, he took several steps back and slinked into the trees to get as far away as he could before Mira told on him. He quickly shifted into his wolf and took off at a dead run in the opposite direction.

Kindal smiled when she saw Mira and looked over her shoulder for Jesse, but he was gone. "Where did Jesse go?" she said out loud.

Jeremiah turned around to see that Kindal was alone. He shrugged and turned back as Mira approached. When she ran right past him, Jeremiah was stunned. He dropped to the ground on all fours and ran after her with Kindal right behind him.

Mira set her sights on Jesse as rage boiled inside her. She thought about how he had chained her up like a dog. The image in her mind fueled her anger, she pushed herself to run faster. She caught up to the black wolf and jumped on his back. She sunk her teeth into the back of his neck and salivated as his blood poured into her mouth.

Jesse's front paws dug into the ground and he skidded to a stop. Mira flipped over his head and landed on the ground in front of him. She jumped to her feet and snarled. Seconds later, Jeremiah and Kindal were there. They both looked back and forth between Mira and Jesse with confused looks as they growled angrily at each other.

Mira took a step toward Jesse and snapped her teeth at him. When Jesse raised his lip and bared his canines at her, Jeremiah jumped between them and growled a warning at him.

Confused and not sure what else to do, Kindal shifted and stood with her hands on her hips beside Jesse. "Okay, what is going on?" she said each word slowly.

Mira growled at Jesse once more before shifting into her human form. Jeremiah hit his head against Jesse's to urge him to shift as well. They both took their human forms at the same time. As soon as Jesse stood up, Mira lunged at him. "You bastard" she yelled as her fist landed hard against his jaw. He stumbled backwards.

Jeremiah grabbed Mira around the waist to stop her from hitting Jesse again. She struggled against his hold. "I'll kill you!" she spat at Jesse.

"What is going on?" Kindal yelled to get everyone's attention.

Mira spared a quick glance in her direction then narrowed her eyes at Jesse. "Your friends don't have a clue who you really are, do they?"

Jesse put an uncomfortable fake smile on his face and tried to act as if he had no idea what Mira was talking about. Kindal looked at him and he shrugged.

"You can stop playing stupid, Jesse" Mira snapped.

"Ok, what the hell is going on here?" Jeremiah growled as Mira squirmed out of his hold.

She took a second to get a good breath then she shook her head. She looked up at Jeremiah, "I don't have time to explain everything right now. Lacey is in trouble, she needs our help. She's with Cole and after I left them, I caught the scents of a group of newcomers. One of them belonged to that Zack guy. I'm sure they've found her by now. We have to hurry."

Jeremiah and Kindal stared at her as if they thought she had lost her mind. "Did you say Lacey is with…Cole?" Jeremiah asked stunned.

"Yes. We have to get to them before it's too late" Mira said in a rush.

"You left her!" Jesse yelled in an accusing tone. "How the hell could you just leave Lacey if you knew Zack was in the area?"

Mira jumped in his face. "Don't you dare try to blame me for a damn thing! This is all your fault. She's out there because of you, not me."

Jesse growled and dropped to the ground on all fours. Without waiting another second, he tore off through the woods. Mira's scent was still strong in the air. All he had to do was follow it back in the direction she came from. But he wasn't alone. He looked over his shoulder and saw Mira and Jeremiah right on his heels. He caught a glimpse of Kindal running off in a different direction, no doubt to get more help.

A million things went through Jesse's mind as he followed Mira's scent. He knew it was over for him. And all his hope of having a life with Lacey was quickly slipping away. Once Mira had a chance to tell Jeremiah what he'd done, everyone was going to turn against him. Maybe even try to kill him.

The smart thing to do would be to leave while he still had the chance too. But he couldn't. He couldn't leave Lacey with Zack. Even though he was sure she hated him now, especially since she was with Cole and most certainly knew what he had done. He had to save her from Zack. No matter what. He loved her too much to walk away.

*****

Lacey looked into the faces of several wolves as they formed a tight circle around her. She tried to sit up but they kept knocking her back down. "What the hell do you want?" she screamed in frustration.

A manly chuckle echoed from nearby. The wolves stepped back from her and sat down. Lacey sat up as Zack came from around a tree a couple feet away. He smiled at her. "It's good to see you again, Lacey. Although I must say, you don't exactly look that great at the moment." He knelt down in front of her and lifted her face with his hand. She jerked away from him and some of the wolves growled.

Zack furrowed his brows as confusion clouded his features. "As a matter of fact, you look a lot like you did as a human. Why is that? I know you're not human anymore. So why do you look so weak?"

"That's none of your damn business" Lacey said. She concentrated hard and tried to pull together as much strength as she could, but her powers were tapped out. She barely had enough strength left to remain conscious.

Zack smiled and brushed her hair back from her face. "You still have your powers, don't you? There is no point in denying it. I felt the power radiating off of you the night Sasha and I came for you. I don't feel it now but I know it's inside you somewhere. That's why you're weak now, isn't it? You've been using your powers. So I guess it's safe to touch you now, huh? Looks like I won't need this after all" he pulled a small pistol from his pack pocket and held it up in front of Lacey. He smiled, "silver tipped bullets. I came prepared this time. But don't worry, I have no intention of killing you. The silver isn't pure."

Lacey narrowed her eyes at him. She wanted more than anything to lash out at him, to be rid of him once and for all. But there was nothing she could do. As she stared at him and tried to think of something to say, the scent of people she knew became detectable in the air. She should have felt relieved knowing that her friends were coming to help her, but she didn't. She felt worse. Because the people coming toward the danger she was in were people she genuinely loved and didn't want to get hurt.

Zack caught the scents and stuck the pistol in his back pocket before grabbing Lacey by the arm and jerking her up from the ground. She wanted to fight against him but she didn't have the strength to. He easily threw her over his shoulder then looked at the small group of six wolves that had become his pack, "don't let anyone follow us. That's an order!"

The wolves all jumped to their feet and growled in unison as if acknowledging the command. Zack took off running. Lacey's head bounced against his back as he ran. She lifted it in time to see Scotty, Luke and Maggie come into sight. The last thing she saw before Zack purposefully hit her head against the side of one of the trees he ran by, was her friends fighting with Zack's pack. Then her eyes closed. She had fought the exhaustion as long as she could but after the blow to her head she couldn't fight it any longer.

*****

Maggie stayed back at a distance while Luke and Scotty charged toward the unwelcomed wolves. She watched nervously as Luke fought with two and Scotty took on three. She didn't see the sixth one as he slinked his way toward her until it was too late. He came up on her side and tackled her to the ground. Catching her off guard, he bit into her shoulder making her yelp out loud.

Luke's head shot up at the sound. Distracted by seeing Maggie pinned to the ground by a much larger wolf, one of his opponents took a bite out of his back leg making him crumple to the ground. His eyes never left Maggie as he quickly got back to his feet and kicked one of the wolves he was fighting. The wolf soared through the air and crashed into a tree. He slid down to the ground where he laid motionlessly.

Before Luke had a chance to run to Maggie, his other opponent jumped on his back. Luke didn't waste any time subduing his enemy. He dug his front paw in the flesh of the wolf's neck and pulled him forward over his head. The wolf crashed on the ground in front of him. Luke quickly bit down on his throat and ripped it open. Blood spurted from the wound and covered his face. It was the first time he had ever killed someone but he didn't have time to feel horrified at what he'd done.

He looked over to see Maggie swipe her paw across the nose of the wolf on top of her. From the corner of his eye he saw Scotty still battling two of the three wolves he had been fighting. The third laid dead at his feet. He darted toward Maggie and knocked the male wolf off of her. They fought briefly and Luke sustained a few wounds but he won the fight when he snapped the other wolf's neck.

Maggie quickly shifted into her human form with tears streaming down her face. Blood covered her arms from where she had been bitten and scratched. Luke resumed his human form and went to her. "Are you alright?" he asked in a panicked voice and looked her over from head to toe to make sure she didn't have any serious wounds.

She nodded and wiped her eyes. "I think so." She glanced over at Scotty as he finished his fight by breaking the neck of one of the wolves while the other ran off into the woods. "But Lacey isn't here. Where is she? Her scent is still so strong in the air" she said in a cracked voice and scanned the trees around them.

"I'll find her. Don't worry, okay. I'm sure she's fine" Luke said and kissed her forehead. Scotty joined them covered in blood and sweat. "I'll go look for Lacey. You just take care of your mate" he said to Luke.

As Scotty was about to walk off, Maggie gasped. She looked up at Luke with surprised eyes. "Do you smell that?" she asked in disbelief.

Luke lifted his nose in the air at the same time Scotty did. They both inhaled deeply. "That's...Cole's scent?" Luke said, unsure whether or not he truly believed what he smelled. "It can't be."

"But it is" Scotty said tensely.

Maggie pulled away from Luke and started to follow the scent. Within seconds, she was running with Luke and Scotty right on her heels. It didn't take them long to find the makeshift cocoon that they were sure Lacey must have made to hide Cole. Luke and Maggie started pulling on the downed trees, but they were bigger and heavier than they could move on their own.

"Help us!" Maggie yelled at Scotty. He stood back, unsure what he should do. He wasn't used to being around people who actually wanted to help Cole. Most feared him and wanted him dead, himself included. But as he watched Maggie and Luke try desperately to move the trees, he fought against the urge to walk away and do nothing, and decided to help them.

After moving several trees from the top of the pile, they were finally able to see Cole looking up at them. They were all surprised by how weak and near death he looked. "Oh God, Cole" Maggie said through the hand that covered her mouth. Tears filled her eyes as she looked at him.

"We're going to get you out of there, Cole" Luke said with certainty.

Cole shook his head. "Help Lacey" he said weakly. "Zack has her."

"What!" Luke and Scotty said in unison.

"Oh no" Maggie said. She grabbed Luke's arm and squeezed as fear settled in her chest. "Please Luke, go find her."

He rested his hand over hers. "I will." He looked over at Scotty, "can you handle this on your own and keep Maggie safe?"

Scotty looked down at Cole and debated on whether or not he really wanted to be involved with saving his life. After a minute, he nodded. "Yeah, don't worry I'll get him out. And I'll watch your girl too. Just call me Mr. Helpful" he said with a bit of sarcasm. "Now go get Lacey."

Luke placed a quick kiss to Maggie's cheek before shifting and running off in the same direction that Zack and Lacey had gone. Left on their own, Maggie and Scotty started working together to remove the rest of the trees surrounding Cole.

CHAPTER FOURTEEN

Jesse couldn't think about anything but Lacey as he stormed through the woods and leapt over the fence that separated the two halves of the mountain. Fear that Zack had hurt her in some way pounded in his chest pushing him to run faster. He tried not to think about Jeremiah and Mira running beside him.

He wanted to be alone when he found Lacey so that he could try and explain himself to her without having Mira screaming about what he'd done to her. But when the woods were suddenly filled with the scents of wolves he didn't know and some that he did, he was thankful to have them by his side to help fight.

When Luke's scent hit Mira's nose, the love of a mother for her son pushed her to run faster. She rushed past Jesse with Jeremiah close behind her. The scents of unknown wolves made her put up her guard. She skidded to a stop when she saw Maggie and Scotty kneeling down on the ground. Relief washed over her when Cole's scent hit her and she knew that it wasn't Luke they were tending to. "Where is my son?" she said after shifting.

Maggie jumped to her feet as Jeremiah shifted and knelt down beside Cole. "Luke went after Zack. He has Lacey" Maggie said in a rushed tone.

From the corner of her eye, Mira saw Jesse standing behind a tree a couple of feet away, no doubt afraid that she was about to rat him out. At the mention of Zack's name, he took off running.

"Get Cole to the village. He needs a doctor" Mira yelled at Jeremiah and the others, "and I'll go after Luke and Lacey." Without waiting for a response, she dropped down on all fours again and darted after Jesse, knowing that they were heading in the same direction.

*****

Lacey opened her eyes slowly as she regained consciousness. Zack was still holding her over his shoulder as he ran. She didn't know how long she was out or how far they were away from her friends but she knew every step he took was another step further away from everyone she loved.

She struggled against Zack. She kicked her legs and started hitting him as hard as she could. A little of her strength had come back, renewing the fight within her. Without even stopping to think about her next move, she struck Zack in the back of the head with her elbow using as much force as she could muster. The blow caught him off guard. Stunned by the impact, he stumbled and fell to the ground. His grip on Lacey loosened, she slipped through his arms and fell to the ground. She landed a few feet away from Zack. Her head hit the ground hard and a wave of dizziness made her temporarily disoriented.

"Bitch!" Zack yelled and jumped to his feet. "You're going to pay for that." He grabbed Lacey by the hair and jerked her up from the ground and slapped her across the face.

The strike was hard enough that it nearly knocked her back to the ground. Lacey stumbled slightly but stayed on her feet. She narrowed her eyes at Zack and licked the blood from her lip. "You better be glad that my powers are exhausted at the moment" she gasped. "Otherwise, you'd be the one bleeding right now."

Zack laughed out loud and pushed her to the ground forcefully. "Oh, I'm not worried about your powers. I will admit that I'm glad you're too weak to use them now because it made taking you a lot easier. But once I get you to your new home; a real nice ten foot by ten foot steel cage that has been plated with sterling silver, your powers will be completely useless in helping you escape." He smiled, cockily. "Sure, you will still be able to hurt me with your powers if you want to, but then there will be no one to take care of you and make sure you have food and substance in your life. So you see, you're going to learn to trust and like me if you want to live. Or else, I'll let you die in that cage."

Lacey's eyes watered as she brought up a mental picture of what he described. She didn't want to live like that – caged, and treated like an animal. That scenario was no better than being locked away in a mental hospital. The thought terrified her. She knew if Zack managed to get her off the mountain her life would be over. She'd rather die right then and there than be his prisoner. She slowly got to her feet using a tree for support. She focused on her wolf and tried to summon her to the surface but just like with her powers, she was too weak to bring her wolf out.

Feeling defeated, Lacey dropped her gaze to the ground. Her eyes landed on a long, thick tree branch by her feet. Zack took a step toward her with his arm outstretched to grab her. In an instant, Lacey ducked down to the ground and grabbed the branch and swung it at him, catching him on the side of the head.

Unfortunately, there wasn't enough force behind the strike to do any damage. He was stunned but not enough to be deterred.

Just as Lacey was about to make a run for it, Zack grabbed her and slammed her against the tree. He grabbed her face and squeezed it roughly. "You are sadly mistaken if you think I am anything like that pathetic bastard Cole. I will not put up with your disobedience. You will learn your place" he snarled.

A grin that looked more natural on Mira's face than Lacey's, slowly pulled up the corner of her mouth. "Oh, I know my place. I'm the alpha female here. I outrank your sorry ass" she said, hoping that she sounded more confident than she felt at that moment. She just couldn't resist the urge to taunt him.

Zack lifted his upper lip and growled. "No bitch is ever going to outrank me. It looks like you need to be taught a lesson" he said and brought his fist back.

Lacey closed her eyes and braced herself for the hit. But it never came. She opened her eyes just in time to see Luke - in his wolf form - leap through the air and tackle Zack.

Relieved to avoid any new pain to her body, Lacey slid down the trunk of the tree to the ground. She wanted desperately to help Luke but there was nothing she could do. She was still too weak to shift or use her powers.

The sound of angry growls and teeth snapping filled the air making her skin crawl. Zack was now in wolf form too.

Lacey looked around hoping that someone else had come with Luke to help him, but there was no one around. Her attention returned to the fight. She grimaced when she saw Zack land a devastating blow to Luke's head with his front paw. His claws dug deep slashes into his flesh. Blood poured from the wounds above Luke's eye making it hard for him to see. Zack took advantage of the situation and charged Luke, clawing and biting him everywhere he could. Lacey screamed for him to stop. They were only a few feet away from her but Zack acted as if he didn't hear her.

Lacey's gaze darted frantically around searching for anything she could use to help Luke. Something black laying on the ground beside Zack's clothes caught her attention. It was the pistol Zack had showed her earlier. She glanced from the gun to Zack as he continued to dominate the fight. Luke was barely able to stay on his feet. Blood covered his fur and dropped to the ground in a steady flow.

Lacey knew he wasn't going to win and that he couldn't take much more. She took a deep breath and pushed away from the tree. She had taken several steps toward the gun before Zack noticed her.

He darted toward the gun shifting into his human form as he snatched it up before Lacey could get to it. He pointed it at her and shook his head with a bloody smile on his face. "I don't think so. You're not fast enough to beat me."

Lacey stood frozen in place and stared at him as a feeling of helplessness washed over her. Zack tilted his head toward Luke, who was laying a few feet away from her in human form. He was alive but bleeding badly from his wounds. "Your friend should have stayed out of our business" he said and smiled again. "I guarantee he won't interfere again." He turned the gun toward Luke.

Lacey's eyes grew wide with fear when she realized what Zack was about to do. Maggie's face flashed in her mind. Losing Luke would destroy her. And Lacey couldn't live with herself if she let him die. He was her friend. Someone she cared about. Someone she loved. Without any thought for her own life, she jumped in the path of the bullet as it exploded from the gun.

The last coherent thing she heard was the popping sound of the gun as it echoed all around her. All the events that followed that awful sound seemed to happen in slow motion.

Seconds after Zack pulled the trigger, he was knocked to the ground by a huge black wolf. Somewhere in the back of Lacey's mind she knew the wolf was Jesse, but the intense burning sensation that filled her chest and spread throughout her body kept her from fully understanding what was happening. She fell backwards through the air and crashed to the ground.

The impact knocked the air from her lungs and gave her double vision. Her eyes fluttered a second before popping wide open. A tortured look crossed her face and a scream erupted from her throat as a torturing pain touch every nerve in her body.

The silver burned in her veins making her fell [feel] as if her insides were literally on fire.

She was in so much agony that she barely noticed Luke when he crawled over to her. He was saying something but she had no idea what. She was too distressed to make sense of anything he said. All she could do was pray that her death would come quickly and the pain would soon stop.

After what seemed like an eternity but was actually only a few seconds, a sinking feeling settled over her and darkness slowly filled her mind. Her screams lowered to a whimper as she started to lose all feeling in her body. The end that she prayed for was finally claiming her.

Her head rolled to the side and she saw another wolf jump into the battle with Zack and Jesse. She barely recognized it through the haze that clouded her mind. It was Mira. That was the last coherent thought Lacey had before she gave in to the darkness that was pulling her into unconsciousness.

"Mom!" Luke yelled as he gently lifted Lacey's head and rested it on his lap. He looked at Mira with tears in his eyes as she stepped away from Zack's lifeless body. Jesse still had his jaws clamped around Zack's throat. "She's barely breathing, mom" Luke cried out.

Mira shifted into human form and hurried to her son's side. Jesse dropped Zack to the ground and quickly shifted as well. He ran over and knelt down beside Lacey. He tried to take her from Luke's arms and Mira pushed his hands away, "back off!" She warned, then ripped Lacey's shirt off to look at her wound. She dabbed her finger in the blood over the hole in Lacey's chest and smelled it. "It's silver" she stated with a shake of her head.

Jesse's face went almost as pale as Lacey's. He stared down at her with sad eyes. "No. No, I can't lose her." His eyes darted from Mira to Luke in a frantic panic, "you have a doctor here right?"

Luke nodded as a single tear slipped from his eye.

"Give her to me!" Jesse growled. He tried to take Lacey from Luke's arms but Mira pushed him back again.

She jumped to her feet and stood in front of Luke while he got to his feet with Lacey in his arms. His wounds were already starting to heal. Mira gritted her teeth and narrowed her eyes at Jesse. "You stay away from her. We don't need or want your help. You've done enough as it is." She looked over her shoulder and nodded for Luke to leave. "Get her out of here. I'll make sure Jesse doesn't follow you."

Luke took off at a dead run. Jesse took a step to follow him but Mira growled and blocked him with her body.

"Get the hell out of my way! I have to be with her and make sure that she's okay" Jesse yelled in frustration.

Mira shook her head and took up a fighting stance. Her whole body vibrated with the urge to make him pay for chaining her up in the cabin. She lifted her upper lip and snarled at him. "If you want to go to her then you're going to have to get past me." She smiled evilly at him. "What's wrong? Are you scared of a fair fight? One where your opponent isn't chained up?"

Jesse balled his hands into fists. "I don't have time for this crap." He tried to sidestep Mira but she was expecting it. She swung her leg out to the side and kicked him in the knee. He lost his footing and she punched him in the back of the head as he fell to the ground.

Mira spun around and waited for him to get back to his feet. Adrenaline coursed through her body in anticipation of a good fight. Jesse stood up and rolled his head around, popping his neck. He growled at Mira, his nostrils flared as he bared his teeth.

Mira smiled. "Let's go. I haven't had a chance to vent my pent up rage in a long time. This should be fun. There's no one here to stop me from killing your sorry ass."

Just as Jesse was about to lunge at her, Jeremiah and Scotty's scents drifted in the air toward them. Jesse looked in the direction their scents were coming from and cussed to himself. "Damn"

Mira raised her brows. "Too bad. I was hoping to have you all to myself" she said teasingly. She took a deep breath, inhaling her mates scent and smiled again. "Jeremiah is on his way. I'd say you have about four maybe five minutes before he gets here. And when he does, I'm going to tell him everything. Although I'm sure he already knows. Cole probably told him everything. You're a dead man, Jesse. You just don't know it yet."

Jesse narrowed his eyes at her and debated his options. His gaze darted from Mira to the woods where he could now hear Jeremiah running toward them. He didn't want to leave. But he didn't want to die either. And he knew if Jeremiah caught him, he would be killed for what he'd done.

With one last look in Mira's direction, Jesse growled at her before dropping to the ground on all fours and darting off at a dead run toward the base of the mountain. By leaving, he'd live another day and have another chance to get Lacey back. *If she made it.*

The thought echoed in his head causing his heart to ache. He didn't want to think about her dying but he knew there was a possibility she would. And it killed him to leave without saying goodbye but he didn't have a choice.

Mira stood staring in the direction Jesse ran. There was no doubt in her mind that he would be back. And she was going to make sure everyone knew to kill first and ask questions second if he ever showed his face on the mountain again. She wasn't a forgiving person and she could hold a grudge for a very long time.

Jeremiah and Scotty rushed from the trees behind Mira, breathing heavily and ready for a fight. Jeremiah stepped in front of Mira and looked around for any threat to her safety but there was none. Scotty ran over to Zack's body and sniffed, then lifted his head in alarm. He scanned the woods with a panicked expression on his face. Seconds later, he and Jeremiah both shifted into their human forms.

"Where is Jesse? He was here. His scent is all over Zack" Scotty said.

"He's gone and if he knows what's good for him, he'll never come back here again" Mira snapped.

Jeremiah wrapped his arms tightly around her waist and pulled her close to his chest. "I was so worried" he breathed into her hair and kissed the top of her head. "Where were you?"

Mira pulled back from him and rested her hand on the side of his face. "Didn't Cole tell you?"

"Cole lost consciousness right after you left. He didn't say anything. We took him to doctor Sims and rushed back here. But why would he know where you've been anyway?" Jeremiah asked, confused.

"And what did you mean by what you said about Jesse? Why is he gone? Where did he go?" Scotty asked. His confusion mirrored Jeremiah's.

"And where is Lacey?" Jeremiah continued with the questions.

Mira lowered her head and let out a deep breath. She wrapped her hand around Jeremiah's. "It's a long, messed up story that I'll tell you about on the way to the village. Lacey has been shot with a silver bullet and Luke took her to get some help. We need to go check on her."

Without saying another word, Mira and Jeremiah shifted into their wolf forms and took off through the woods, leaving Scotty standing by Zack's body looking like he had no clue what was going on. His gaze flickered from the direction Mira ran to and the direction that he could sense Jesse's scent in. He stood there for several minutes unsure of what he should do…follow Jesse or go back to the village and check on Lacey.

He felt pulled in two different directions. They were both his friends and he wanted to make sure they were okay. But he couldn't go in two directions at once. After a few more minutes of thought, he fell to the ground on all fours and ran after Mira and Jeremiah.

He had to know that Lacey was going to be alright and he was confident Jesse could take care of himself. But more importantly, he wanted to hear the story that Mira was going to tell Jeremiah, especially since apparently it had something to do with Jesse. Maybe it would explain his strange behavior.

CHAPTER FIFTEEN

Luke pushed through the crowd of his pack members outside the doctor's cabin with Lacey in his arms. Everyone had already heard about Cole being alive and were there to see him. "Move!" Luke yelled to clear a path to the door. "Get the hell out of the way!"

The crowd quickly separated, giving him access to the porch. Being exhausted from fighting and then running several miles with Lacey unconscious in his arms, Luke stumbled on the bottom step. He lost his grip on Lacey and she slipped from his arms. Just as she was about to hit the ground, a second pair of hands caught her.

Luke looked thankfully at Dean as he lifted Lacey up to his chest and carried her the rest of the way up the steps and into the cabin.

Relieved to see that Luke was alright, Maggie rushed over to him and wrapped her arm around his waist and helped him up the steps. They followed Dean inside the Doc's cabin.

"Put her down on the couch" the aging pack doctor ordered from the corner of the room as he washed blood from his hands.

Dean gently laid Lacey down and backed away. His eyes roamed the room until he saw Cole laying unconscious on a bed by the wall. The blood on the doctor's hands had come from him. Both of his legs were cut open with metal braces attached to his bones. Dean quickly looked away. He had seen some of his friends with the same contraption on their legs and sometimes even their arms when they had broken bones. Re-breaking and connecting the bones properly was how they healed but Dean's friends never looked as lifeless as Cole did.

"Doc! Help her!" Maggie yelled through tears as she knelt down beside Lacey. Blood covered her chest and steadily oozed from the gunshot wound.

Doctor Sims hurried to the couch and began examining Lacey. He had a grim look on his face as he checked her. He ran from the room and came back with a black leather bag. "I need everyone to leave" he said and sat down on a small table by the couch and began pulling operating tools from his bag.

Maggie grabbed a hold of Lacey's hand and squeezed it tightly. "I want to stay with her" she pleaded.

The doctor glanced at her with sympathy in his eyes. "I'm sorry, but you can't." He sighed, "I won't lie to you, Maggie. She might not make it. I think the bullet pierced her heart. That, combined with the silver…" he shook his head sadly, "well it doesn't look good. The longer the bullet stays in her body, the worse it's going to be. I need to get to work. Please leave so I can try to save her."

Maggie's whole body started shaking as the doctors words sunk in. Sobs built in her chest. "No!" she screamed. "She can't die."

Luke wrapped his arms around her from behind and lifted her up. It broke his heart to see her so distraught. He hugged her tightly to his chest as tears filled his eyes. "We have to go" he whispered against her hair and moved backwards toward the door.

Maggie struggled against him as he pulled her far enough away that her hand slipped from Lacey's. "Luke, please don't. I need to stay with her. She's my friend!" she yelled through her sobs.

Luke closed his eyes against the wave of grief creeping up on him. "I know, baby. I know" he said softly and tightened his grip on her. Against her will, he pulled her out of the cabin. Dean followed and shut the door behind them, leaving the doctor alone to do his work.

Once outside, Maggie collapsed on the porch. Luke tried to comfort her as she cried for the only friend she ever had. Dean left them to tell the rest of the pack what was going on.

*****

Five hours passed before the door of the doctor's cabin finally opened and he stepped out onto the porch looking worn out. The entire pack was still waiting outside for an update. Jeremiah, Kindal, Scotty and Mira had joined the crowd right after Maggie and Luke were forced out of the cabin.

Jeremiah jumped up from his seat on the porch beside Luke and Maggie. "How are they? Are they going to make it?" he asked anxiously.

Doctor Sims rubbed his hand through his thin white hair and let out a deep breath. "I've reset the broken bones in Cole's legs and I'm giving him fluids for the severe dehydration. He's badly malnourished and very weak. And he has an infection but he is going to make it. His body just needs time to heal. He should be back to his full strength in a few days."

"What about Lacey?" Maggie asked in a hoarse voice, her throat was dry from all the crying she'd done. Luke helped her stand up with his arm around her waist.

The doctor met her eyes briefly before looking out at the rest of the pack. "I retrieved the bullet from her chest but I was correct when I assumed it had nicked her heart. I did my best to repair the damage but the silver infected her blood stream and it's preventing her from healing the way she should" he paused, "she's fighting for her life right now. And she's very lucky the silver in the bullet wasn't pure. It was diluted with metal and copper, which weakened it."

"So, she's going to be alright then?" Luke asked.

"I don't know" the doctor answered honestly. "Any of the rest of us probably could have handled being shot with the bullet used on her with nothing more than being sick for a few days. But Lacey was already in a very weakened state before she got shot. Her powers had drained her, making her body more susceptible to the effects of the silver. All we can do now is wait and see what happens."

Everyone was quiet for a while as they took in the news. A few sniffles and murmurs broke the silence. Kindal, who had been standing at the end of the porch with Scotty, angrily brushed the back of her hand across her cheek to wipe away her tears. "So that's it? We just wait and hope she lives? Is that the best you can do? She's your freaking alpha female and that's the best you can do for her?" she yelled.

The doctor turned his attention to Kindal. He frowned, "I'm sorry. I've done all that I can. It's up to her now. She has to fight it."

Kindal took a step toward him. A growl built in her throat, threatening to choke her. "That's not good enough" she cried. Scotty grabbed her by the arm and pulled her back to him. He wrapped his arms around her and held her to his chest in a tight embrace to console and also restrain her. "She'll be okay, Kindal" he whispered in her ear to calm her down. "Lacey's a fighter, you know that. She's going to make it. We just have to believe that, okay." She nodded against his chest.

The doctor cleared his throat and rested his hand on Jeremiah's arm. "Cole will be waking up soon" he paused and looked uncomfortable if not nervous, "I may need some help to keep him calm, especially when he sees Lacey. I'm just an old man, I won't be able to control him if he loses it when he finds out what happened to her."

"Don't worry. I'll stay with him" Jeremiah said. The doctor nodded his thanks.

"Can I stay too?" Maggie asked, hopeful.

"I don't think that's a good idea" Jeremiah said before the doctor could answer. "The doc's right. Things are going to be tense when Cole wakes up. It's best that no one else is here."

"But…"

"No buts, Maggie" Mira said softly, "Just listen to Jeremiah and I give you my word that I'll send for you as soon as Lacey is conscious."

Maggie looked stunned that Mira had spoken to her with something other than hatred in her voice. She met her eyes and when she did, Maggie saw something that she had never seen on her before. Sadness. Mira actually looked sad and almost caring for once. Maggie wasn't sure if it was an act or if she really did feel something for Lacey, but now wasn't the time to question her motives. "You promise?" Maggie asked.

"Yes" Mira confirmed. "Now go home and get some rest" she paused and looked at Luke before dropping her gaze back to Maggie, "and take care of my son. He's had a long day. He needs his future mate to take care of him."

Luke smiled at Mira and gave her a hug. "I love you, mom."

"I love you too. Now get Maggie out of here. She looks exhausted." Mira pushed him toward the steps. Without another word, Luke and Maggie left, as did everyone else but Jeremiah, Mira, Kindal and Scotty.

Jeremiah followed Doctor Sims inside. When Scotty and Kindal started for the door, Mira stepped in front of them. "We need to talk. It's time I tell you the truth about Jesse. Come on, we can talk at my cabin."

Scotty and Kindal passed confused looks to each other, then reluctantly followed Mira down the steps of the porch and into the woods.

*****

Jeremiah was asleep in a chair by the front door of the doctor's cabin when he was awakened by someone grunting. He opened his eyes and looked around the darkened room. The sun had disappeared hours ago and the door to the doc's bedroom was closed. Movement by the wall caught his attention. He jumped up from his chair when he saw Cole sit up on the bed.

"Don't try to get up" Jeremiah said and hurried across the room, tripping over a table along the way. He put his hands on Cole's chest and tried to push him back down on the bed.

Cole swatted him away. "Leave me alone." He squinted his eyes against the dark and tried to focus on his legs. The metal brackets the doctor had put on them when he first arrived at the cabin were no longer there. His legs were now encased in temporary casts.

Knowing that Cole still wasn't a hundred percent and that his senses weren't back to normal yet, Jeremiah flipped the light switch on so he could see better. "The doc did a good job on you. Before he went to bed, he checked on you and said that the infection you had is almost completely gone. He also said you could probably take the casts off in the morning. You're healing really fast, especially with the fluids and everything else he's been giving you." He pointed to the IV in Cole's arm.

Cole ran his hands down his face and swung his legs over the side of the bed as if he was going to stand up. "I feel a hell-of-a-lot better." He breathed in deeply and let out a heavy breath then froze deathly still. His eyes met Jeremiah's. "Where is Lacey? She's here. I smell her scent. Why isn't she here with me?" He looked around Jeremiah and searched the room. There was no one else there.

Jeremiah looked nervous when an alarmed look crossed Cole's face. "Where the hell is she?" Cole asked again with an edge to his voice.

"She's here, Cole. Just calm down" Jeremiah said.

"The hell I will. I want to see Lacey now." Cole grabbed ahold of the casts around his lower legs and ripped them off. The white plaster molds fell to the floor in pieces.

He then pulled the I.V from his arm and dropped his feet down to the floor. He was a bit wobbly at first when he tried to stand so he leaned against the bed to support himself. After a minute he was able to stand on his own. He started across the room. His first steps were slow and unsteady but they quickly increased in speed as his heart raced in his chest in anticipation of seeing Lacey. He pushed past Jeremiah and stumbled toward the closed door where Lacey's scent was coming from.

Jeremiah rushed ahead of Cole and blocked the door with his body. He looked at his cousin with caution. "Before you go in there just listen to me, okay. You have to know that the doc did everything he could to help her."

Cole's brow furrowed in confusion. "What? What the hell are you talking about? Get out of my way!" he said as fear made his chest feel tight.

Jeremiah turned the knob and pushed the door open. Cole stood in the doorway with his eyes fixed on the bed in the middle of the room. A thick lump formed in his throat almost preventing him from speaking. "Wha…what happened?" he asked in barely more than a whisper. His eyes were locked onto Lacey's motionless body.

Jeremiah leaned against the doorframe with his arms crossed over his chest. "Zack shot her with a bullet laced with silver."

Cole's eyes instantly widened. He balled his hands into fists before turning and punching a hole in the wall behind him. He leaned his head against the wall for several seconds and breathed deeply to try and calm himself. "Is she going to live?" he asked in a shaky voice.

"We don't know. Doc said the bullet nicked her heart but that it wasn't enough to kill her. Neither is the amount of silver in her body. But the two combined with how weak she was before she was shot, makes it much more difficult for her to heal herself" Jeremiah said gently.

"And Zack? Where is that little bastard?" Cole growled and pushed away from the wall and made his way over to the bed. His chest ached as he looked down at Lacey, pale and unmoving. He reached a shaky hand out to touch her.

"He's dead. And so are all of the others he brought with him." Jeremiah followed Cole to the bed. He rested his hands on the footboard and approached the next subject he needed to talk about very cautiously. "And Jesse's gone. After he and Mira killed Zack, he ran off." He paused and shook his head sadly, "I'm sorry, Cole. I'm sorry that we didn't look harder for you. But we just didn't think Jesse…"

"It's not your fault" Cole interrupted him. "You can leave now" he said in a low voice as he stared at Lacey.

Jeremiah looked at him. He knew the calm on his face was just a mask to cover how he was really feeling. "Cole, you don't need to be alone right now. Let me stay with you until…"

"Don't you dare say it! Don't you say until she dies because that's not going to happen. Do you hear me?" Cole yelled in a cracked voice. "I won't let her die." He shook his head and lowered his voice, "she can't die because I can't live without her" he whispered and ran his hand down the side of her face.

Jeremiah stood silent as he watched one of the strongest men he had ever known crumple to pieces in front of him. When Cole lifted Lacey's head and cradled it to his chest and started crying, Jeremiah couldn't take it anymore. He had never seen Cole shed a single tear before. There was a time when he didn't think it was physically possible for him to cry. But as he watched him now, he knew that he had been wrong. Everyone had been wrong about Cole. He did have a heart. It just took a very special woman to find it. And now it was breaking.

Unable to watch Cole crumple to pieces in front of him, Jeremiah quietly left the room and eased the door closed behind him. He hurried through the cabin and out the front door. The need to hold his own mate in his arms hit him like a freight train. He still had the love of his life and he needed her now more than ever. He couldn't help but think about how close he came to losing her. The thought of being in Cole's shoes and having to watch the woman he loved die caused a massive pain to shoot across Jeremiah's chest. He dropped to the ground on all fours and ran all the way home.

CHAPTER SIXTEEN

Cole opened his heavy lids and looked across the bed at Lacey. He had spent the whole night by her side and still there was no change. He could smell the silver in her blood as it coursed through her body. The difference in her condition and the condition Mira had been in when she was stabbed with a silver dagger was devastating.

When Mira was infected with silver, she had spent days withering and screaming in pain as her body fought against it. But Lacey wasn't moving or talking at all. It was like she was in a coma. And to Cole, that was much worse than seeing her struggle in agony. At least if she was screaming, he would know that there was hope she was going to make it. But she did nothing…she just laid there.

Cole rested his hand on her chest, over her heart. He could feel it beating. And he knew she was still hanging on but he didn't know how much longer she could keep fighting. He laid his head on her chest as sharp pains ripped through his heart at the thought she may never open her eyes again. And that he might never again see her smile. He closed his eyes and drifted off to the dream world he had created in his mind.

A world where he and Lacey were together, running through the woods in their wolf forms, playing without a care or worry in the world. It was just them and the love they shared. After a few minutes, his dream vision changed to them standing in front of the mating alter in human form.

Lacey was wearing the blue satin dress she had picked out for the mating ceremony. Her beautiful long blond hair was put up in an elegant up-do. Her eyes sparkled like sapphires as she smiled at him. That was the way he wished she looked now.

Happy and full of life. Cole forced reality from his mind and submerged himself deeper into his dream world.

*****

Several times over the next few days, people knocked on the door to Lacey's room. But each time, Cole yelled for them to go away. He only allowed the doctor to come in to check on Lacey but each time the news was the same. And after each visit Cole became more distraught. He was beginning to lose hope.

When Lacey finally opened her eyes twelve hours later as he rubbed a cool, wet rag across her forehead to help relief her fever, Cole was so surprised to see her looking up at him that he forgot how to breathe. "Lacey" he gasped and dropped the rag.

It took a lot of effort, but she managed to force a small smile to her face. Her body felt as if it was on fire, burning from the inside out. She wanted to scream from the pain, but she forced herself to remain silent. From the look on Cole's face, it was clear that he had been through enough and she didn't want to hurt him more by making him watch her suffer.

She knew the pain consuming her body was from the silver. She could feel it as it coursed through her blood. But she also knew that her body was fighting against it. She was getting her strength back, but it wasn't enough to keep her conscious. Before she could say anything to Cole, she drifted back to sleep. At least then she didn't have to feel the pain anymore. She welcomed the darkness and the peace it brought with it.

*****

Almost an entire day passed before Lacey woke up completely and was able to stay awake for more than a few minutes. Each time her eyes opened, the first person she saw was Cole. He never left her side and it was seeing his face every time her eyes opened that kept her fighting. The burning sensation that had tortured her for what seemed like an eternity was finally gone.

Lacey took a deep breath as the last of her pain faded. Her body had won the fight against the silver. She looked at Cole asleep beside her on the bed. He looked exhausted. She had no idea how much time had passed since she was shot but it felt like days, maybe even weeks. And from the rough way Cole looked, he hadn't slept much during that time. She leaned over and kissed him on the cheek before sitting up in the bed.

At first, she felt a little dizzy but as she sat there, the feeling faded. She got out of bed and stood for a second to make sure she wasn't going to lose her balance and fall. She was surprised at how steady she was on her feet. Her strength was coming back faster than she expected it to. She looked down at Cole, relieved to see that his wrists and legs had already healed. A shiver ran down her spine at the memory of how they looked when she first found him.

The different scents that filled the cabin caught Lacey's attention. She inhaled deeply and sprinted toward the bedroom door. Anxiety had her nerves on edge. She swung the door opened and stared teary-eyed at the faces looking back at her. She was so relieved to see her friends alive and unharmed. Her eyes landed on Luke and happiness filled her heart to see that he was okay.

Maggie jumped up from the couch and lunged toward Lacey. She grabbed her in such a tight hug that she could barely breathe.

"Maggie" Lacey gasped and tapped her arm to get her to loosen her grip. "Can't breathe."

Everyone in the room laughed. Luke playfully pried Maggie's arms from Lacey and kissed her on the cheek. "She's really happy to see you" he said to Lacey.

"And so are the rest of us" Jeremiah said as he and Mira approached her. "It's good to see you up and walking around."

Lacey smiled. "It's good to be up. I feel like I've been sleeping forever."

"Four days" Mira said. "It's been four very long days."

"Too long" a familiar voice said from across the room.

Lacey looked past Mira to see Dean leaning against the wall. His freckled face lit up when Lacey smiled at him. "But I do have good news" he said as he crossed the room and gave her a small hug. "I finished the cabin" he whispered in her ear so no one else could hear.

Lacey surprised everyone in the room when she grabbed Dean and kissed him on the cheek. "Oh, that's great news! Thank you" she said and kissed him again before pulling him close for another hug.

"Am I missing something?" Luke asked as he looked between Dean and Lacey.

"Dean, did you forget that Cole didn't actually die and is in the next room?" Maggie asked with a hint of annoyance and sarcasm. "Do you have a death wish or something? If not, I suggest you drop your hand from Lacey's waist before it gets ripped off."

Before Dean could respond, a deep, rough voice sounded from the room behind him. "She's got a point, kid. You might want to listen to her."

Everyone in the room tensed. Lacey dropped her arms from Dean's neck and spun around to face the man standing behind her. Her heart leapt in her chest when she saw Cole staring at her with the same desire that was erupting within her. In that moment as their eyes met, no one else existed. It was just him and her. And the burning need she had to be close to him. To hold him and never let him go. They had both survived the unimaginable and she desperately needed to feel him against her skin.

She closed the small distance between them and jumped on him. Too lost in the moment to care about her audience, she wrapped her legs around his waist and started kissing him.

Chuckles from Jeremiah and Luke echoed in the cabin, while Maggie dropped her eyes to the floor, a dark blush crept across her cheeks.

"Oh hell, this is not something I want to see" Mira said and tried to hide her smile as she walked out of the cabin, shaking her head.

Cole and Lacey continued kissing. She tightened her legs around his waist as he spun her around so that her back was to the wall. Things were getting really heated. Cole broke from the kiss and glanced over his shoulder at his unwanted guest. "Out! All of you!" he growled in a rough, breathy voice.

"You don't have to tell me twice" Dean said and hurried out the door. Jeremiah followed him, laughing all the way outside.

Maggie looked uncomfortable as she and Luke headed for the door. She stopped and glanced back at Cole and Lacey. She quickly dropped her eyes when she saw Lacey reach for the zipper on his jeans. "Um, shouldn't you guys wait until you're mated?" she said cautiously.

"Out Maggie!" Lacey yelled in between kisses.

Maggie opened her mouth to argue that waiting was the right thing to do, but Luke smiled at her and shook his head. "No point in trying to make them see the error of their ways when their bodies aren't being controlled by their brains at the moment." He laughed and pushed Maggie out the door.

Cole wrapped his arms around Lacey to hold her in place as he walked across the cabin and kicked the door to the doctor's room open. Doctor Sims was sitting at his desk. He looked up with alarm.

"Get out, doc" Cole said and nodded toward the door as Lacey kissed his neck, making a throaty growl escape his lips.

"What?" The doctor asked as he stood up. "This is my cabin" he said defensively.

"Not today it isn't" Cole said, ignoring the wide-eyed look the doc gave him.

Lacey slid down the length of his body until her feet touched the floor. She lifted her shirt over her head and tossed it across the room. Her eyes never left Cole as she spoke to the doctor with her back to him, "I appreciate everything you've done for us doc, but please leave. Don't make me have to throw you out." She used her mind to toss the vase from his desk out the window to get his attention.

"Enough said. I'll come back later or maybe tomorrow" Doctor Sims said and quickly ran out of the cabin.

Cole looked at Lacey, "you've changed. I can sense it, you're tougher than you used to be" he said.

"That's what happens when you lose the one person you love more than anything in the world" Lacey said in a tight voice.

Cole pulled her to him and crushed his lips to hers. "You didn't lose me. I'm still here" he said and lifted her up in his arms, "and I always will be."

He carried her into the other room and laid her down on the bed. He lowered his body on top of hers with his weight supported by his elbows. "I love you, Lacey."

She grabbed his face and pulled him down to her so she could kiss him. Within minutes, the fire inside her intensified to the point she couldn't take it anymore. The need to be with him was overwhelming. It overpowered everything else in her mind. She pushed at his chest until he rolled over onto the mattress beside her.

He looked at her with his raised brows and a seductive grin on his face as if daring her to take the lead. "Are you sure you're ready for this?" he asked.

Lacey growled playfully and jumped on top of him. She could feel her powers trying to surface as her emotions grew more excited. She tightened her hold on them and pushed them to the back of her mind. She didn't need her powers or her wolf at the moment. For once, she was going to let her heart take control of her actions. "Absolutely" she said and seductively bit down on her bottom lip.

*****

Time stood still as their bodies joined and moved together as if they were specifically made for each other. Everything was perfect. Every touch. Every kiss. Every movement. Nothing in either of their lives had ever made them feel as complete as they felt at that moment, wrapped in each other's arms, drowning in ecstasy.

All of the heartache they'd suffered over the last weeks was washed away, replaced by a love so intense that it was impossible to contain. It fueled their desire, making them cling to each other even more, unwilling to let go of the pleasure erupting within them.

The bond that formed between them as they made each other's fantasies come true was stronger than anything Lacey had ever felt. She knew that having sex with Cole didn't make him her mate, but it was impossible to imagine a bond even more powerful than the one she already felt with him. A deep, sensual growl rumbled in his chest as she scraped her nails down his back. She loved that sound and did everything she could to make sure he kept making it for several hours.

*****

Cole and Lacey laid naked in each other's arms, enjoying the sated feeling that followed great sex. They were both tired, but in a good way.

Lacey lifted her head from Cole's shoulder and brushed her damp hair back from her face. She smiled and slowly drew circles across his chest with her finger. "Do you have any idea how happy I am right now?" Her smile faltered, "I mean, a few days ago I was on the verge of insanity. I had actually forgotten what it felt like to feel anything but heartache. But now, I'm on top of the world. It's amazing how things can change so quickly."

Hearing Lacey talk about how she felt while he was away seared a hole in Cole's heart. The whole time he was trapped in Jesse's makeshift prison, it never entered his mind that Lacey was suffering the way she was. He'd assumed, with Jesse's help of course, that she had accepted his death and moved on with her life. It wasn't until Mira told him the truth that he understood how much Lacey really loved him. And how close he came to losing her to her own instability.

He was shocked when he learned what she'd done to Dallas in the village, the way she used her powers on him, nearly killing him. And how she destroyed their cabin, leaving nothing but the floor intact. Cole's chest tightened as he thought about how unstable she had become. He wanted to make sure nothing like that ever happened again.

He cradled Lacey's face in his hands and stared into her eyes. "I am so sorry for everything that happened while I was gone. I'm back now and I'm not going anywhere without you ever again. I swear no matter what, we stick together" he paused, "but you have to give me your word that if one day something does happen to me you won't lose the control that I know you have over your powers now. You're a powerful woman, Lacey. You can destroy everything and everyone we know and I don't want that to happen. So promise me you'll never lose control again. I wouldn't ask this of you if I didn't think you could make this promise and keep it, but I know you can."

Lacey pulled away from him with alarm in her eyes. "What do you mean if something happens to you? Nothing is going to happen to you. You said that our kind lives a very long time, over a hundred years."

"We do" Cole said to calm her, "but we aren't immortal, Lacey. One day we will die, and if I go before you, I don't want our family and friends to suffer because of your powers. So promise me you'll keep control."

Lacey closed her eyes as tears slipped through her lashes. She didn't want to think about them dying, especially not when they just found their way back to each other. But she knew Cole was right. She could never again allow herself to be as out of control as she was the night she destroyed their cabin. Too many innocent lives would be at stake. "I promise" she said and threw herself into his waiting arms. "I'm sorry for what I did to Dallas, the cabin, the way I treated everyone over the last few weeks. I was just hurting so much."

"I know, baby. But it's all over now, okay. We're back together now and we always will be" Cole whispered and rubbed his hand down her back to soothe her. He held her like that for a while, neither saying a word, just enjoying being together.

It wasn't until Lacey's stomach growled like a lion, that Cole remembered she hadn't eaten in four days. A smile stretched across his face as he released his hold on her and got out of bed.

"Where are you going?" Lacey asked as she watched him pull his jeans on.

"To get you something to eat." He glanced out the window across the room to see that it was pitch black outside. They hadn't been paying much attention to the time. "How does a late dinner or early breakfast in bed sound? I'm sure the doc has something in the kitchen I can fix for you...or" he raised his brows playfully, "we can try your luck at hunting again. Your first attempt was so entertaining, I can't wait to see your second try" he teased.

Lacey grabbed the pillow from behind her and threw it at his head. He caught it and held it to his nose, breathing in her scent. He smiled and tossed it back on the bed. "So is that a no? You don't want to go hunting? Are you still trying to deny your wolf its basic instincts?"

Lacey rolled her eyes and tightened the sheet around her chest before getting out of bed. She approached Cole and grabbed him around the neck with one hand and released the sheet with the other and went for the zipper on his jeans. "I don't deny my wolf anything anymore. And what she wants now, is you" she said and pulled his head down to hers and kissed him roughly.

Cole didn't need any further prompting. He was more than willing to satisfy the hunger he saw in her eyes that had nothing to do with wanting food. He scooped Lacey up in his arms and carried her back to bed where they stayed for the rest of the night.

CHAPTER SEVENTEEN

Movement in the room woke Lacey from a light sleep. She stretched out across the bed, reveling in how good her body felt. It was almost as if the last week never happened. All of her strength had come back. She could feel her wolf lingering just under the skin. And her powers were ever present in the back of her mind.

"I didn't mean to wake you" Cole said from across the room.

Lacey sat up in bed and smiled at him as he put his boots on. "You didn't. Where are you going?"

Cole finished with his shoes and sat down on the bed beside her. "Last night was the most amazing night of my life and I would love to stay here in bed with you for the next several days, but we have work to do," he sighed and rubbed his thumb across her cheek tenderly, "A lot has happened around here. We need to get things back in order. Let the pack know everything is fine, and that we're up to the task of leading them." He frowned a little, "and let's not forget that this is the doc's cabin. Ours…" he paused and shook his head with a small grin, "needs major work done to it before it's going to be habitable again thanks to a certain temperamental little wolf girl."

Embarrassed, Lacey covered her face with her hands. Cole chuckled and pulled her hands away so that he could kiss her. She smiled and Cole raised his brows when he noticed the sneaky look that crossed her face.

Lacey jumped out of bed and grabbed her clothes from the floor. "I've got a surprise for you. One that will solve our housing issue." She quickly got dressed and opened the bedroom door. "Are you coming?" she asked over her shoulder and stepped out of the room.

There were lots of things that needed to be discussed about everything that had happened, but at the moment nothing seemed more important than seeing the smile Lacey hoped her surprise would bring to Cole's face.

He grinned suspiciously and followed her outside. "Lacey, what are you up to?"

She took his hand in hers and tugged him through the village, smiling and waving at their pack members that were out and about. "You'll see. Just follow me" she said and released his hand and started running toward the trees at the far end of the village.

Cole smiled and took off after her, enjoying the playfulness of the moment. As he chased her through the woods he couldn't help but notice where they were going. So when Lacey skidded to a stop a short distance from his childhood home, he wasn't that surprised. However, he was a little stunned when she spun around and demanded that he close his eyes before going any further.

"What?"

"You heard me. Close your eyes. Take my hand and I'll lead you the rest of the way" Lacey said sternly.

Cole looked at her with curiosity then tried to peek around her to see whatever she was trying to hide from him. She popped him on the arm playfully and pouted her lips. "Stop it! You can't see it from here anyway so just play along. I know you like games" she said with raised brows, hinting at his past and the way they met. "So close your eyes and play my game. I really want this to be a surprise."

"Alright" Cole said reluctantly and eased his eyes closed. Lacey took his hand and he opened one eye and smiled at her, "just so you know this is a first for me. I've never allowed myself to be led blindly into anything. I hope you know how big of a milestone this is for me and how much trust I have in you."

"I do" Lacey said with a smile and squeezed his hand. Cole closed his eye and let her lead him through the woods. When she stopped walking and he heard her gasp, his eyes shot open with alarm. He wasn't prepared for what he saw. Lacey was standing a few feet in front of him staring at the cabin that used to be nothing more than a run-downed shack.

Cole was speechless as he stared at the cabin he grew up in, all fixed up just the way he remembered it from when he was a child. He was bombarded with emotion and unable to believe his eyes.

"Do you like it?" Lacey asked as happy tears slipped from her eyes.

"I…I love it" Cole stuttered as he walked toward the cabin. He climbed the steps of the porch, rubbing his hand over the new logs that formed the banister. He reached for the door knob and froze. He was excited but at the same time afraid to look inside. A part of him wanted everything to look the same as it did when his parents were alive but another part of him didn't.

The rational side wanted everything to look totally different so that he wasn't reminded of the past and the pain it carried with it. But the small sentimental side of him wanted to remember it the way it used to be when his mother would sing while cooking dinner in their old yellow kitchen.

Cole stood still with his hand wrapped around the knob trying to sort through the many different emotions soaring through him. Lacey came up behind him and eased one arm around his waist and rested her other hand over his on the doorknob. She kissed his shoulder tenderly, "it's alright Cole, just let the past go. Let this moment be the beginning of your future. The start of our new life together."

Cole closed his eyes and leaned his head against hers as the sincerity of her words washed over him, comforting him, urging him to let go of the bad memories so that he could make new ones with her.

Letting go of the pain he'd carried with him for so long seemed impossible to do, but when Lacey whispered, "I love you" in his ear, he knew that he could do it. As long as he had her by his side, he could do anything. And it was that thought that forced his hand to turn the knob.

He pushed the door open and stood in the doorway with his arm wrapped around Lacey's waist. They both looked around the newly remodeled cabin with smiles on their faces. Cole kissed the side of Lacey's head, "this is perfect" he said as his eyes wondered around the room that looked nothing like it did when he was a child.

The furnishings and décor was a perfect mixture of his and Lacey's personalities. The dark colors on the walls, the sleek wooden furniture and bar-style kitchen was the complete opposite of what had been inside his parent's home.

Lacey nodded in agreement. "It is perfect. Dean did an excellent job. This place already feels like home to me and we haven't even gone inside yet."

"So, is this what all the hugging and kissing with Dean was about?" Cole asked.

She smiled. "Yes. I was just thanking him for all of his hard work. And I must say that I'm very proud of you for not losing your temper."

Cole frowned. "Well, let's just say that after being on the receiving end of someone else's wrathful side, I've taken a second look at how I treat people."

Lacey knew that he was talking about Jesse and once again, she wanted to ask him about what had happened between them for the two weeks he was missing. But the hard, deep in thought look on his face let her know that it wasn't the right time yet. She tightened her arm around his waist and squeezed him closer.

Cole smiled and urged her forward. Once inside, they split up to explore the cabin. Lacey went to the bedroom and Cole headed into the kitchen. Something on the back wall caught his eye. His chest tightened when he saw the plaque that his father had made, hanging in the same place it had always hung. It had been cleaned up and a dark stain had been brushed over it to make it look new. But it was still the same plaque.

He reached out and rubbed his hand over the words 'home sweet home' and for the first time ever, his heart didn't hurt when he thought about his father. Instead of remembering his death, he remembered the day he helped his father carve the plaque. He remembered the smile on his father's face as they laughed together. He remembered the joy he had felt as he watched his father carve each and every letter with love for his family. That was what he was going to remember from now on. The good things not the bad.

Lacey startled him when she wrapped her arms around him from behind. "We're going to be so happy here. I can feel it."

Cole turned around in her arms and cradled her face in his hands. "I agree" he said and lowered his mouth to hers.

Their kiss was sweet, slow and full of passion. It was in that moment, standing in their new home, with the man she loved in her arms, that Lacey decided she wasn't going to let another minute pass by without being forever bonded to him.

Her heart raced in her chest as she broke from their kiss. Fear and excitement filled her at the thought of finally being able to complete the ceremony that she'd wanted so long for. She looked at Cole from under heavy lashes with a timid smile. "I want to be mated to you now. As in right now. Not later today, not after Maggie and Mira put up meaningless decorations, not after Jeremiah organizes a grand feast but right now at this very moment."

Cole stared into her eyes, searching for any doubt that she might have about spending the rest of her life with him, but there was none. All he saw was absolute devotion and love for him. He didn't deserve it, and truly thought he would never find it, but with Lacey, he had found his redemption. She had saved him from himself and showed him how to love again. And for that, he would be forever thankful to have her in his life. "Are you sure this is what you really want, Lacey?" he asked in a soft voice.

She kissed him again. "More than anything in the world. I don't ever want to take the chance of losing you again. And I don't need a fancy ceremony. All I need is you."

"Alright then" Cole said and took her hand in his. He led her into the bedroom. They sat down side by side on the bed, both of them nervous. Cole gave her a shy smile, "I have a confession to make. I've never actually been to a mating ceremony before. I always skipped out on them when I was a child. So I don't know the words to the vow we are supposed to say" he said with embarrassment.

"Then we'll make our own vows" Lacey said and turned around on the bed to face him. She slipped her shirt over her head and dropped it to the bed then did the same with Cole's. She grabbed his hand and placed it on her bare chest. Her eyes met his and she held his gaze. "This is all that matters. How we feel here" she pushed his hand down over her heart. "The truth is there are no words to fully describe how you make me feel. When I'm with you, I feel whole, complete. The emptiness that I've felt my entire life disappears. The loneliness that used to make me cry myself to sleep at night, doesn't exist anymore.

And the wounds of my past don't hurt as much because I know if you can love me then my parents could have too, but they chose not to." She paused, "I'm happy with you, Cole. When I thought I'd lost you…" she sighed and wiped the tears from her eyes, "all I felt was pain. It was even hard to breathe. I felt like my chest was being crushed by the weight of my broken heart. When you let go of my hand and I saw you fall from the cliff, I lost a part of myself, the part that made life worth living. But I have it back now and I don't ever want to lose it again."

Cole blinked back the tears that threatened to surface. He hated himself for hurting her so badly. He pulled Lacey to his chest and hugged her tightly. "I am so sorry, baby" he said and kissed the top of her head. "I swear I will spend the rest of my life making sure you never feel that way again. I promise."

Lacey lifted her head from his chest and placed her hand over his heart. "And I promise to spend the rest of my life doing everything I can to make you happy" she said and reached her hand into the back pocket of her jeans and pulled out the small pocket knife she'd taken from the doctor's cabin. She looked down at it, then up at Cole, "looks like we've taken care of the vow part."

He smiled and kissed her gently, "I guess we have, haven't we?" His gaze dropped to the knife in her hand, "do you want to go first or do you want me to?"

Lacey let out a deep, relaxing breath. "I think I'll go first just so I don't lose my nerve" she joked with a nervous chuckle.

"Alright" Cole took the knife from her and opened it before giving it back. He guided her hand to his chest with the tip of the knife placed over his heart. Her hand was shaking. "Don't worry about me. I won't feel a thing. The cut doesn't have to be deep, just enough to draw blood" he said to encourage her.

Lacey looked at him apprehensively and nodded. "Okay. I can do this" she said to herself to build up her courage.

After taking another deep breath, she sliced the blade across his skin then quickly opened a gash in her own hand. She clamped her jaw tight as the blade pierced her skin and a burning sensation spread throughout her palm. She closed her fist around the wound to keep the blood from spilling on the bed. Then she handed the knife to Cole and stuck her chest out in expectation of the cut she was about to receive.

In the span of a second it was over. She felt the tiny sting as the blade cut through the skin over her heart. Warmth spread throughout her body when Cole placed his bleeding hand over her wound. And she did the same to him. With their hands firmly pressed over each other's heart, their blood mixed and a new, distinct scent filled the room. Lacey stared wide-eyed at Cole as the bond between them formed.

It was an instant connection, magical in way. Like his blood was calling out to hers, pulling her closer, binding their lives and souls together. Lacey gasped from the force of emotion that suddenly consumed her. In that moment she felt what Cole felt. The joy and bliss that filled his heart. She could feel his wolf as well as her own, begging to be released so that they could claim each other.

Unwilling to deny the request of her other half, Lacey dropped her hand from Cole's chest and kissed him before allowing her wolf to take over. She didn't know if it was what she was supposed to do or not, but it felt right.

Cole followed her lead and shifted into his wolf form so that they could consummate their mating in the traditional way, as wolves. There were no barriers between them as their basic instincts took over and the two wolves became one.

*****

"How do you know they're at Cole's parent's cabin?" Maggie asked Luke as they walked through the woods toward the newly remodeled cabin.

"I know because Dean told me he saw Lacey dragging Cole through the village earlier today in this direction. He also told me that Lacey had asked him to fix up the old cabin for her. They have to be there. Where else could they be?" Luke said with a smile.

"Well, I really hope she is there because I'm going to give her an earful about that little stunt of hers yesterday" Maggie said in a stern tone. "I can't believe she slept with Cole before being mated to him. I mean, I know you don't have to be mated to have sex, but I just think it would have been more special for her if she had waited."

"You mean you wanted her to be more like you. Traditional" Luke said and squeezed her hand.

Maggie lifted her gaze to meet his eyes. "So what if I did. Was it wrong for me to want to have something in common with her? We're so different in every other way."

"No, it wasn't wrong to want that. But you're wrong about being different. You have a lot more in common with Lacey than you think. She's strong-willed, determined, a fighter, and sometimes stubborn, but she has a good heart and so do you. All of those other qualities apply to you too."

Maggie smiled. "I guess we're more alike than I thought. I don't know about being a fighter or the stubborn part, but I guess I agree with the rest."

Luke laughed and shook his head. "Trust me, you can definitely be stubborn. Especially when it comes to the people you care about. But that's one of the things I love most about you" he said and kissed her cheek.

They stepped from the trees into the small clearing in front of the cabin they were looking for. "Wow" Maggie said as she stared at Cole and Lacey's new home. "It's beautiful."

All of the weeds and bushes that had grown up the sides the last time she saw the cabin had been removed. The logs on the porch looked new. The windows were definitely new and the flowers that lined the front of the cabin were the reddest Maggie had ever seen.

"Let's see if they're home" Luke said and urged Maggie up the steps. He knocked on the door and waited. The sound of footsteps hurrying across the floor on the other side brought a smile to Maggie's face. "They're here" she gushed excitedly.

Seconds later, the door swung open and Cole was standing in front of them wearing nothing but a pair of jeans. His chest glistened with sweat. "What's up?" he asked with a grin.

The scent that flowed in the air from the cabin caused Maggie's mouth to drop open. Her eyes widened as she stared at Cole. Anger quickly lit up her features. "You didn't!" she yelled and raised her hand to poke him in the chest, like a chastising little sister. "How could you? How could you have the mating ceremony without telling us?"

Luke immediately grabbed Maggie and pulled her back before the punch she threw had a chance to connect with Cole's jaw.

Cole tried to hide the grin pulling up the corners of his mouth while he watched the feisty little blond swinging her fists at him. She definitely wasn't the same sweet, shy girl he had met when he first arrived. A little of Lacey's attitude had rubbed off on her.

Just then, Lacey appeared in the doorway behind Cole. She took one look at the angry look on Maggie's face and cringed. She knew she was about to get it. She braced herself for the torrent of screams she expected to hear. But instead of yelling,

Maggie looked at her with tears in her eyes then turned and walked away without saying a word. They were all stunned by her action. Luke started after her and Lacey stopped him. "No. Just go inside and talk with Cole. I'll go talk to Maggie."

Reluctantly, Luke followed Cole inside and closed the door. Lacey jumped from the porch and ran to catch up with Maggie as she was about to enter the woods. "Maggie, wait" she said and grabbed her arm.

Maggie spun around with tears streaming down her face. "What!" she yelled.

Lacey flinched at the harshness of her voice. "What's wrong, Maggie? Why are you so upset?"

She wiped her hand angrily across her cheeks and shook her head. "Nothing. I'm fine. Okay. I have to go." She turned around to leave but Lacey quickly moved to block her path. "I can't let you leave until you tell me what's wrong. You're my friend Maggie, and I care about you. I don't like seeing you hurt like this."

"Then why wasn't I invited to your mating ceremony?" Maggie snapped and crossed her arms over her chest. "I really wanted to be there for you. I've never..." she stopped without finishing her sentence.

Lacey could tell that there was more to Maggie's breakdown than she wanted to talk about. "You've never what, Maggie?"

She looked away for several minutes. When she finally looked back at Lacey, years worth of pain was visible on her face. "I've never been involved in the preparation of a mating ceremony before. To our kind, the ceremony is the most honored celebration that we have. Just look at it like a human wedding, you have the maid of honor and bridesmaids, even a best man. Well, it's the same thing with a mating ceremony. Your closest friends are the ones chosen to stand by you to help out with everything. And I've always wanted to be one of the lucky ones that got chosen, but I never have been because I've never had a real friend until you. I know it's selfish of me, but I really wanted to stand beside you in front of the whole pack to show them all that you chose *me* to be there for you."

"Oh Maggie, I'm sorry. I really am. But we didn't have a real ceremony, it was just Cole and me. I didn't know how much this meant to you" she said and hugged Maggie. "But if it'll make you feel better, we'll have a formal ceremony to celebrate the fact that Cole and I are already mated and invite everyone. I'll even let you fix me up like a doll if you want to. Just don't be mad at me, please."

Maggie thought about the offer briefly, then smiled. "I'd like that. But I think I'd like you by my side at my mating ceremony even more." She smiled, "the date's been set. I turned eighteen two days ago. Luke and I are going to be mated six weeks from today."

"Oh my God, Maggie that's great!" Lacey beamed and hugged her again. "But I'm sorry I missed your birthday."

She shrugged. "It was no big deal. No one but Luke knew about it and he made me a delicious strawberry cake. Besides, you have a good excuse for missing it…you know, being shot and unconscious for four days" she said with a hint of sarcasm and a smile.

"Are we good now?" Lacey asked with hope in her voice.

"Yeah, we're good. I'm sorry that I overreacted" Maggie said and leaned her head on Lacey's shoulder as they headed back to the cabin. "This new scent of yours is going to take some getting used to though. It's kind of weird. I mean, I know that once two people become mates their scents mix and become one but the new scent is usually closer to that of the male before he became mated, with only a hint of the female's old scent. With you and Cole, this new scent has more of your old one than his."

Lacey took a second to think about what she said. "Huh, what do you think that means?" she asked curiously.

"I have no idea. Maybe that you're the dominate one in the relationship?"

Lacey raised her brows and laughed, "Yeah right. Try telling that to Cole. On second thought, don't. I like it when he thinks he's in control."

Maggie laughed out loud as they made their way back to the cabin. The door opened as soon as they stepped foot on the porch. Cole and Luke stood in the doorway staring at them like they expected them to start fighting or something.

Lacey rolled her eyes and pushed past them, tugging Maggie behind her. She smiled to herself when she heard Cole whisper to Luke, "I told you there was nothing to worry about."

"Me?" Luke whispered back, "I wasn't the one who wanted to rush out and drag them both inside. That was you, my friend."

Cole ignored him and went to stand beside Lacey. He eased his arm around her waist and smiled at Maggie. "You still want to rip my head off for mating with Lacey without your permission, little girl?" he teased.

Before she could respond, Lacey answered for her. "No, she doesn't. However, we do have a celebration to plan now." She paused to take in the confused look on Cole's face then continued, "technically, we're already mates so there is no need for us to have a ceremony, but we should have a get-together and invite our pack to help us celebrate our mating."

"Uh-hum" Maggie cleared her throat, "formal celebration" she clarified, "not a get-together or cookout. A real celebration, as in a fancy party. Well, as fancy as it can get here on the mountain. But you get the point."

Cole glanced back and forth between Maggie and Lacey, amusement lit up his eyes. "If that's what it takes to make you girls happy, then I guess we're going to have a party."

The four of them sat down to discuss arrangements for the upcoming event.

CHAPTER EIGHTEEN

The next few days were very busy for Lacey and Cole. They had finally settled into their new home and fell into the roles as the alpha leaders fairly quickly. Most of the pack was thrilled to learn that they had already become mates, but there were some who were disappointed. Mostly females who Lacey thought had been hoping to catch Cole's eye sooner or later.

All of the arrangements for their party had already been made and things were finally getting back to normal. The only difference being that Lacey was spending a lot more time with Mira. They had surprisingly become close over the last few weeks.

When Lacey was told that Scotty and Kindal had left the mountain once they learned she had awoken from her coma, she was a little hurt and confused. She couldn't believe they left without saying goodbye. But considering the circumstances and the fact that everyone on the mountain was looking for a way to get back at Jesse for what he'd done, she knew it was for the best that they had left. Otherwise, her friends, who she was certain couldn't possibly have been involved with Cole being held captive and beaten for weeks, would have been the ones forced to pay the price for Jesse's actions. Cole's kidnapping was all anyone on the mountain wanted to talk about. No one could believe what Jesse had done to him.

Lacey tried several times to talk to Cole about what had happened when he was locked up, but each time he changed the subject by saying that it was in the past and he didn't want to talk about it. So Lacey had no choice but to seek out the only other person who knew what had happened in the abandoned cabin.

Mira had been reluctant to talk to her at first considering the promise she'd made to Cole about keeping his mental state at the cabin a secret. But with the possibility that Jesse could return one day, Mira felt that she had no choice but to tell Lacey what she knew. So she told her how Jesse beat and tortured Cole with lies about being with her, telling him how in love they were and that they were going to be mated.

The more Mira talked, the angrier Lacey became. She couldn't believe how blind she'd been. She blamed herself for everything that happened to Cole. If only she had seen through Jesse and made him tell her the truth, then Cole wouldn't have suffered so much. And the sadness in his eyes that she saw whenever he thought no one was looking wouldn't be there. He didn't want to admit it but Lacey knew he was hurting. And it had nothing to do with her.

She kept her eyes on him all the time and after a while she began to figure out what was bothering him. Every time Jesse's name was mentioned, a pained look crossed his face. He quickly covered it with a blank expression, but Lacey had seen the hurt in his eyes. Whether he wanted to admit it or not, and as crazy as it seemed, she couldn't help but think that before Jesse imprisoned him, Cole had still cared for his brother.

They had fought with each other for decades, but neither of them had ever actually physically harmed the other until now. The more Lacey thought about it, the more her theory made sense. At any time over the last twenty years, Cole could have easily killed Jesse in retaliation of their father's death if he wanted to, but he didn't. Instead, he let him live. That said a lot about how Cole really felt about him.

*****

Maggie smiled at Lacey's reflection in the mirror over her new vanity. She had been working on her hair and makeup for over an hour in preparation for the party. "You look beautiful" she said and squeezed her shoulders before glancing around the room, "and so does this bathroom. Your new cabin is amazing. I hope mine and Luke's looks half as nice as this one."

"Well from what I hear, Dean and the others started work on it today, with the hopes of having it done in time for your mating ceremony in a few weeks" Lacey said and brushed some of the newly curled hair from her face. "I was told that starting from scratch takes longer than just fixing up an existing cabin."

"I really hope it's ready before the ceremony. That'll be one less thing I have to worry about" Maggie said and began fidgeting with her dress.

Lacey turned around on the stool to face her. She could sense a change in her with the new topic of discussion. "Is everything alright with you and Luke?"

Maggie's eyes shot open wide. "Oh yes, we're fine. Great actually."

"Then what's all the nervousness I sense coming from you about?" Lacey asked with raised brows.

Maggie was quiet for several seconds as she twisted the hem of her dress around her fingers. "I don't know. I mean, I really do love Luke and I want to become his mate, but I'm scared. I don't know if I'm ready for all of this." She paused and looked down at the knotted mess she was making with her dress. "Once I'm mated, things between Luke and I are going to change. There will be no reason for us to wait any longer. He's going to expect things from me that I don't know if I'm going to be good at…"

Lacey looked at her thoughtfully. "Are you talking about sex?"

Maggie nodded her head shyly as a blush crept across her cheeks.

"Aw Maggie, there is no reason to worry about that" Lacey said reassuringly. "Luke loves you and I don't think he's going to expect anything from you. He's a good man. He'll wait until you're ready and when you both decide the time is right, it'll be amazing for both of you."

"You think so?" Maggie asked timidly.

"Yeah. I know so" Lacey said and hugged her. "No more worrying, okay?"

Maggie smiled. "Okay" She looked at their reflections in the mirror once more and fluffed up a few of Lacey's curls. "We need to get going. The celebration is about to start. Jeremiah said that we should be in the village by six, and it's already ten minutes till." She nudged Lacey with her elbow playfully, "it wouldn't be polite for the guests of honor to show up late."

Lacey smiled, "Cole's already there. I'm sure he will make up a story to cover for us." She sighed, "I can't wait to see the surprise he left earlier to go get. Do you have any idea what it is?" she asked Maggie.

"I don't have a clue, but I do know that Luke rode into the city with Cole to get it this afternoon. Mira was fussing about them leaving because she didn't think they would be back in time for the party. I was so relieved when I saw them in the village helping with decorations on my way here. It must have been a really fast trip. I asked Luke what Cole went to get and he just smiled and shook his head because he knew I would tell you."

Lacey rolled her eyes and smiled. "He's right, you would have."

"I know" Maggie agreed and pushed Lacey toward the door. "Time to party."

They left the cabin and started toward the village. The darkness engulfed them as they entered the woods. It wasn't a long walk, maybe half a mile. But in heels and dresses, it was going to take them a little while to get there. They had only walked a short distance when Lacey abruptly stopped. "I forgot something" she said and looked over her shoulder, back toward the cabin.

"What?" Maggie asked.

"I have a gift for Cole and I want to give it to him at the party. It's nothing fancy, just something I made but it means a lot to me. I have to go back and get it."

Maggie shook her head as Lacey turned around and started walking back toward the cabin. "Lacey, we don't have time for you to go back. We're already late. Cole is probably going crazy wondering what's taking so long."

"Go on to the village and let him know that I'm on my way" she yelled and started a slow jog. "I'll be right behind you."

"Lacey, this isn't a good idea" Maggie yelled but she was already out of sight. "She never listens" Maggie said to herself and resumed her walk toward the village.

*****

Cole was leaned against one of the many tables spaced throughout the open area of the village. He looked out over the crowd at his pack members dancing and having a good time. The music that filled the air combined with the smell of the food cooking was intoxicating. He searched the crowd looking for Lacey, but he didn't see her anywhere.

"She'll be here. Stop worrying."

Cole glanced to his right and saw Mira standing beside him with a know-it-all grin on her face. He shook his head and let out a deep sigh before smiling at her. It was strange how much their relationship had changed.

There was a time when they couldn't stand each other, now they were slowly becoming friends. Both of them had let their guards down while they were trapped together and showed that neither was as hard and tough as they appeared to be. It made them understand each other better. "Who says I'm worrying?" Cole asked innocently.

Mira offered him a beer. "It's written all over your face. You look like a dog who has lost his bone. Lacey is your mate now, you don't have to worry about anyone taking her away. So just relax, and enjoy the party. She's probably still letting Maggie treat her like a human Barbie, I actually feel a little sorry for her" she teased.

Cole chuckled at the thought. He knew that Maggie had indeed insisted she be the one to make Lacey presentable for the party. He relaxed a bit and took a sip of his beer. Luke and Jeremiah joined them with a tray of barbequed meat and hamburger buns. "Let's eat" Luke said and sat down at the picnic table.

Cole laughed and popped him on the back gently. "Maggie is going to kill you. You know that, right? I do believe her orders were no cook-out food or beer" he held up his drink and nodded toward the can, "total elegance was what she said, and I'm not real sure what that means but it's what you agreed to when she asked you to take care of the food for the party."

Luke took a big bite of his burger and smiled. "This is my version of elegance. There is nothing better than my dad's barbeque and everyone here knows it" he said in his defense.

"Oh no, son, you are not bringing me into this" Jeremiah said with a light chuckle. "You asked for barbeque so I cooked it, but you never said anything about Maggie wanting a higher standard of food. This one is on you" he paused and looked toward the crowd. Maggie's scent drifted in the air toward them. "And it looks like you're in for a hell of a night, son. She looks pissed" he said and pointed in Maggie's direction as she forced a path through the dancing bodies of her pack mates.

She stopped a few feet in front of the table where everyone was sitting. Her arms were folded tightly across her chest as she narrowed her eyes at Luke. He dropped his burger to the plate. Cole lowered his head and laughed quietly to himself. "Take it like a man" he whispered to Luke before getting up from the table. He smiled at Maggie and gave her a brief hug, "give him hell" he said teasingly.

"Oh, I intend to" she said and pouted her lips angrily. Cole laughed again and glanced around her, searching. "Where is Lacey?" he asked when he didn't see her.

The angry look instantly fell from Maggie's face. "She had to go back to the cabin for something. She'll be here soon."

A worried look creased the corners of Cole's eyes. "She shouldn't be walking around in the woods alone. I'm going to go get her" he said and started away from the table. He didn't make it more than a few steps before he was jolted to a stop.

The scent flowing in the air toward him made his entire body instantly tense up. He looked over his shoulder to see that Jeremiah and everyone else had caught the scent as well. Within seconds, Mira, Luke, and Jeremiah were at his side with the same hard look on their faces that Cole had on his. Maggie stayed back behind them. "Where is she?" Luke growled.

Mira lifted her nose in the air and breathed deeply. "She's coming from that direction," she pointed toward the woods closest to them, "she's very close."

A minute later, Kindal stepped from the woods. The entire village stood frozen, the music from the band stopped and everyone turned toward her. "What are you doing back here?" Mira snarled at her. "When I told you about Jesse, you made the decision to leave and I told you if you did, not to ever come back."

"I know" Kindal said breathlessly, like she had been running for a very long time. She approached Cole and tried to catch her breath. "I didn't have a choice. I had to come back. Jesse has really lost his mind. He's not himself. He said that if he couldn't have Lacey then neither could you" she said to Cole. "He's coming for her. She's in danger…" before she could finish her sentence, Cole took off at a dead run toward his cabin.

The chaos that followed happened too fast to describe. Within seconds, Cole's entire pack shifted into their wolf forms and tore off after him.

*****

Lacey rushed up the steps of the porch and hurried inside to grab Cole's gift. The instant Jesse's scent hit her nose, she froze. She spun around in the middle of the living room, glancing in every corner of the cabin. "I know you're in here, Jesse. Where are you?" she asked nervously.

The bedroom door eased open and Jesse stood against the door frame with a heart-broken glare on his face. His eyes met hers and a shiver went down her spine. He looked nothing like the man she used to know and love. In front of her stood the monster that everyone had always claimed Cole was.

Jesse's hair was dirty and disheveled. The stress lines that creased his forehead aged him and made him look cruel. Lacey began to panic. "What are you doing here? How can you come back here after what you've done?"

Jesse pushed away from the doorframe and took a staggering step toward her like a drunk man. "I came for you. But I'm too late now, aren't I?" he spat and swung his arm out and knocked the lamp off a small end table as he passed by it. "You're his mate now. You mixed your blood with his. You let that bastard touch you…" he said disgustedly and glanced around the room. "You turned my mother's home into a sick little love nest."

"That's none of your business, Jesse. Get out!" Lacey ordered sternly and pointed to the door. Her voice faltered when her powers forced their way to the front of her mind, catching her off guard and making her momentarily dizzy.

She had worked so hard over the last couple of weeks to learn how to control her powers and be able to force them away and summon them at will. This time, they came out of nowhere. She clamped her jaw tightly against the strain on her mind and forced her powers back.

She didn't want Jesse in her cabin and was honestly afraid of him at the moment but she could not allow herself to use her powers against him. She couldn't break the promise she had made to Cole, no matter what.

Lacey took several steps backwards as Jesse made his way toward her. He could see the stress on her face and feel the tension radiating from her body as it shivered. "All I ever wanted was you, that's it. Before you came into my life I never knew how lonely I was. I'd lived my life doing a job - protecting humans from my brother. I never even bothered to try and find a mate or someone that I could love. I wasn't happy but I'd accepted that as my life. Then I saw you" he chuckled bitterly to himself, "a helpless human stealing fruit to eat. I knew the moment I saw your face that you were different. That you were special."

Lacey kept her eyes locked on him as he spoke. She slowly inched around the room trying to get as close to the front door as possible.

"I tried so hard to fight my attraction to you," Jesse continued, "But as I watched you struggle and fight with your powers, I saw how strong you were and I could feel the pain in your heart when you talked about your parents. I knew I couldn't fight it anymore. And once I opened my heart to you, everything changed. I fell in love with you. I thought you loved me too, but you didn't, did you? It was all a lie. You played me" he said in a rough, accusatory voice and narrowed his eyes at her.

"That's not true" Lacey said defensively, and took another step toward the door. Jesse jumped in front of her and grabbed her shoulders. Before she could react, a sharp sting pierced the skin on the side of her neck. She blinked wide-eyed at him as she sagged in his arms. "I did love you" she gasped softly as her head fell against his chest and her eyes fluttered closed.

Jesse let the needle fall from his hand with a little of the sedative still inside it. He hated to drug her, but he knew it was the only way to stop her from fighting back. It was another trick he'd learned from his brother.

He scooped Lacey up in his arms and looked down at her. Regret filled him as he stared at her painted pink lips, the urge to kiss her rocked him to his core. "I'm sorry," he said even though he knew she couldn't hear him. His heart ached at the thought of what he was about to do, but his mind was made up. He stormed from the cabin with Lacey in his arms. Their final destination wasn't far away.

CHAPTER NINETEEN

Cole's feet pounded up the steps of the porch. The door of his cabin was wide open. He ran inside. "Lacey?" he called out to her as he stood motionlessly just inside the doorway. Fear crippled him and made it difficult to breathe. Jesse's scent was thick in the air. "Lacey!" he screamed her name and forced himself to move. He ran from room to room searching for her.

Back in the living room, his eyes landed on the needle lying on the floor by the end of the couch. He bent down and picked it up. Alarm spread throughout his body when he held it to his nose and smelled it. A rough growl rumbled in his chest. He knew Lacey was incapacitated. Wherever she was, she was unable to fight back. To protect herself. Knowing she was defenseless filled Cole with so much rage that his entire body began to tremble.

He crushed the needle in his hand and dropped to the floor on all fours. His skin gave way to black fur as he darted outside. Within seconds, he caught Lacey's scent in the air. He inhaled it deeply then threw his head back and howled several times to vent some of the rage boiling inside him. Then he leapt from the porch and ran into the woods behind the cabin, in the same direction that he'd gone the night he followed Jesse the first time he tried to take Lacey. The night he fell over the cliff.

A sense of déjà vu filled him and he growled at the memory, then pushed it from his mind and forced himself to run faster. Jesse and Lacey's scents were getting closer. The muscles in his legs burned and ached as he pushed himself even harder. His bones had healed but his muscles were still weak from lack of constant exercise.

Cole skidded to a stop and lifted his nose in the air when the direction of Lacey's scent changed. He sniffed and started running again, straight toward the cliff that had nearly ended his life. He ran as hard as he could. When the cliff came into sight, he stopped so abruptly that his back legs flipped over his head and he crashed to the ground. He scrambled to his feet, desperation clear on his face as he stared at Jesse. Unable to believe what he saw, he quickly shifted into his human form.

"Jesse! Don't!" Cole yelled as he rushed toward him.

Jesse was standing at the edge of the cliff with Lacey unconscious in his arms. He spun around at the sound of Cole's voice. "Don't come any closer" he warned and took a small step backwards.

Cole instantly froze. All the rage that had been boiling over inside him a moment ago vanished, an immense fear had taken its place. He held his hands up in front of him to plead with Jesse, "move away from the edge, Jesse. You might fall."

A dark chuckle answered, "that's the whole point of standing this close." Jesse sighed and shook his head sadly, "this isn't what I want to do but I don't have a choice." He looked over his shoulder at the sheer drop behind him. "It's kind of ironic, don't you think? The last time we were here, both of us were dangling over the edge, desperately wanting to live. Now instead of wanting to live, I want to die." He paused and looked down at Lacey as tears swelled in his eyes. "Things didn't turn out so good for me. You got your happy ending, you got Lacey. But I'm not going to let you keep her."

Cole's heart sank to his feet. He shook his head as panic settled in his chest, making it hard to breathe. "Jesse, please don't do this" he pleaded, his voice on the verge of cracking. "Just give her to me. I give you my word, I'll let you leave without anyone harming you. You can leave, go back to your friends and have a good life. You'll find another woman to fall in love with. Just please give Lacey to me."

The pain and emptiness inside Jesse prevented him from even considering Cole's offer. He looked at his brother with a sad grin, "you don't get it, do you? There is no one else for me. Just like there is no one else for you. I guess we are more alike than I thought. We both fell in love with the same woman" he sighed sadly, "I might have lost her in this life, but I'll have her forever in the next." He lowered his head and kissed Lacey on the forehead.

She squirmed in his arms as she started to regain consciousness. She opened her eyes and looked up at him, her vision blurred.

"I love you" Jesse whispered and squeezed her tight to his body. Without giving her a chance to respond, he closed his eyes and threw himself backwards, over the cliff. Cole yelled and leapt through the air toward him.

Air rushed passed Jesse as he fell backwards. A smile crossed his face as a sense of satisfaction consumed him. But it was quickly snatched away when Lacey was ripped from his arms. His eyes sprung open at the loss of her body next to his. An immense pain shot through his right arm as his fall was jolted to a stop and he was jerked upwards.

Jesse gritted his teeth against the pain and looked up into Cole's strained face. He was laying on his stomach in the same position Lacey had been in when she was trying to save them weeks earlier. Both of Cole's arms were over the edge of the cliff. One of his hands was wrapped tightly around Lacey's wrist and the other was around Jesse's.

"Just hold on!" Cole grunted as he tightened the muscles in his arms and began slowly pulling them up.

Jesse looked at Cole in disbelief then let his eyes fall to Lacey, dangling from Cole's other arm a few feet away. She was wide awake now and fear was etched in every feature of her face. "Cole" she called out to him as tears rolled down her cheek.

"I got you, baby" he said in a strained voice. "Just hold on."

She looked down at the roaring water below her and gasped. She tried to find leverage against the side of the cliff with her legs, but there was nowhere to put her feet. "Please hurry" she cried when she felt herself slipping from his grip.

Cole dug his feet into the ground behind him to hold himself in place. "Climb up my arm, Lacey!" he shouted at her.

She grabbed ahold of his arm with her other hand and started pulling herself up. She was almost to the top of the cliff when Jesse grabbed one of her legs. She screamed when he started pulling her back down. She kicked at him with her other leg.

"Damn it, Jesse. Let her go!" Cole yelled.

Lacey kicked her leg again, hitting Jesse in the face. He dropped his hand from her leg. And she quickly pulled herself the rest of the way up. She grabbed a hold of Cole's shoulder and climbed over the side of the cliff. Once Cole was sure she was safely on firm ground beside him, he let go of her wrist and looked down at Jesse, dangling from his arm.

"Just let me go" Jesse said.

"No. Never" Cole growled and reached for him with his free hand. Jesse swatted his hand away and shook his head. He pulled against the hold Cole had around his wrist. His skin burned and his flesh ached. He could feel himself slipping free as the weight of his body pulled him downward. He smiled sadly, "this is the way it was meant to be. I can't live without her," he said and glanced at Lacey as she looked over the edge at him, "I'll tell mom you said hey."

Those were the last words Jesse spoke before he jerked himself free of Cole's grasp and fell over a hundred feet to his death.

"No!" Cole screamed and grasped at thin air. Lacey tugged him away from the edge.

Jesse was gone. And Cole looked as if he wanted to jump over the cliff after him. The total devastation and shock that covered his face proved that Lacey had been correct in thinking he still cared about his brother.

"He…he's gone" Cole muttered as he stared into the empty space in front of him. "My brother is gone" his voice cracked. He slowly shook his head from side to side as one tear after another rolled down his cheeks.

Lacey stared at Cole as her own tears flowed. She didn't know what to say. He looked like he was in shock. When his eyes met hers, she gasped from the pain that she saw in them. She threw her arms around his neck and held him as tightly as she could. His body began to shake and he leaned heavily against her, needing her to support him as he crumpled to pieces over the death of the brother he claimed to have hated.

Lacey felt completely and utterly helpless. Cole clung to her, his tears flowed freely and uninhibited. She wanted to comfort him, to say something to ease his pain, but there were no words that could ease the pain of losing a family member.

When some of their pack members came from the trees toward them, Lacey shook her head and motioned for them to leave. Jeremiah shifted into his human form and stood at the tree line. Their eyes met briefly and he knew something really bad had happened. When his gaze dropped to Cole, clinging to Lacey like a small child, he knew the danger was over and that Jesse was dead. He lowered his head and left them to grieve, making sure that the rest of the pack followed his lead.

*****

Hours passed before Cole and Lacey made their way back to their cabin. Neither of them said a word as they walked hand in hand through the woods. It wasn't until Lacey started up the steps of the porch that Cole finally spoke.

"Where are you going?" he asked, his voice hoarse and dry.

Lacey looked at him, confused. "We're home. Let's go inside. You need to rest."

Cole shook his head. "No. We have a party to attend."

Lacey stared at him, unable to believe what he said. She was starting to get worried that he was suffering from some kind of mental breakdown or something. She rested her hand on the side of his face and stared into his eyes. "Cole, let's go inside. You're in no condition to party."

Cole rested his hand over hers and squeezed it gently. His eyes were bloodshot and swollen. "If losing my brother tonight has taught me anything, it's that I don't ever want to waste a moment of our time together." He sighed and looked away as Jesse's face popped into his mind. "Because we never know when our last moment will come" he said sadly.

Lacey was quiet for a few minutes as she studied his face. "You did love him, didn't you? After all these years and all the fighting, you still loved him" she said, certain that she was right.

A tear slipped from his eye and rolled down his cheek. "I wanted to hate him. I tried so hard to and sometimes, I really did hate him. But he was my brother." He sighed and wiped at his eyes. "Jesse did hate me though. And his hatred wasn't forced either, it's what he really felt for me. Fighting with him was the only way I could keep some kind of contact with him."

Lacey shook her head sympathetically. "So all these years,

you instigated fights with him just so you could have him in your life in some form? Why didn't you just tell him how you felt?"

"Because I knew he hated me and there was no point in telling him how I felt." He sighed sadly, "and with every innocent human that I killed or had killed, his hatred of me grew even more. I've never blamed him for how he felt. I deserved his hatred. But I guess I got to the point that I didn't care anymore."

"Oh, baby" Lacey said and threw her arms around Cole in a tight embrace. "I'm so sorry we couldn't save him."

He returned her hug, holding her tight as he closed his eyes and moved around in a small circle. Lacey couldn't believe her ears when he started humming the song they had danced to the night at the bonfire. She knew he was crying as he hummed, she could feel his tears on her shoulder, but she didn't say anything. She just closed her eyes and hummed along with him as they slow danced. She couldn't help but feel like Cole needed that moment to help him heal his broken heart.

*****

The next couple of weeks were tense and emotional, but Cole and Lacey got through it together and their bond grew even stronger. They had both been shocked to learn that shortly before Jesse showed up the night he died, he had gotten into a fight with Scotty and nearly killed him. And it was after that fight that Kindal had come to warn Cole.

Apparently Jesse had attacked Scotty when he told him that what he did to Cole and Mira wasn't right. And that he should just leave Cole and Lacey alone. His disapproval was not something Jesse wanted to hear. Luckily, Scotty survived the fight and was now back on the mountain. When Kindal didn't return, he came looking for her. And after a long talk with Kindal and Lacey, he decided to stay.

Kindal refused to go back to Carol Springs now that Jesse was gone. She said that she'd rather stay with Lacey, especially since Trevor and their old pack were upset with them for not going back weeks ago when Trevor left. And Scotty couldn't bring himself to leave her there alone. He knew Lacey wouldn't let anything happen to her but he decided to stay anyway.

They both fit in well with their new friends. Scotty had already caught the eyes of several females, with hopes of making him break his vow of bachelorhood. And Kindal had surprisingly developed a crush on Dean.

After a long overdue talk, Lacey learned that the guy Kindal had been seeing, Steven, had left the pack shortly after she fled with Cole. No one had seen or heard anything from him since. Lacey was relieved to know that she was no longer with him, and so was Kindal when Cole told her what he knew about Steven.

With the craziness on the mountain finally dying down, things started to return to normal. The biggest news flying around now was the upcoming mating ceremony for Luke and Maggie. Mira had personally taken it upon herself to get involved and make sure that it's the grandest ceremony ever conducted.

Luke and Jeremiah were overwhelmed by all of Mira's instructions but Maggie was happier than anyone had ever seen her. She enjoyed the attention she was getting from Mira and everyone else. And Lacey and Cole enjoyed not being the center of attention for once.

They spent most of their time alone at the cabin making up for lost time and ensuring that they never lose another moment of their time together.

*****

Cole set a warm plate of spaghetti and meatballs down on the table in front of Lacey. She looked at it but made no move to take a bite.

"Is something wrong with it?" Cole asked and examined the food on her plate.

"No. It's just that I've been thinking that maybe I want to try my luck at hunting again" she said and lifted her eyes to his with a small smile on her lips. Her gaze dropped to the hand-made leather bracelet around his wrist that she had made for him. It was the gift she had gone back to the cabin to get the night Jesse died.

"Really" Cole said, a huge grin spread across his face. "And what may I ask has brought this change on? Every time I've mentioned going hunting in the last two weeks, your reply has been a firm 'no'. What's changed?" he asked curiously.

Lacey tried to hide the smile on her face with her hand. Her latest visit with Doc Sims had confirmed the suspicion that she'd had for over a week. She was just a few weeks away from her nineteenth birthday and her life was about to get even more complicated than it had been in the last year. But as scared as she was, she felt nothing but overwhelming joy at the future ahead of her.

She dropped her hand from her mouth and stood up, feeling playful. "What? Can't a woman change her mind if she wants to?" she said teasingly and brushed her body up against Cole's as she slid passed him on the way to the door. "Besides, aren't you the one who keeps telling me that I should embrace my wolf's natural instincts and let her hunt?"

Cole eyed her suspiciously. He didn't want to let on that he already knew her secret. He enjoyed watching her play with him. But he knew the truth about why she wanted to go hunting. Her body was changing and so were her needs. He smiled and joined her on the porch. She was unbuttoning her shirt, getting ready to shift. He came up behind her and wrapped his arms around her waist with one of his hands balled into a fist.

"What's in your hand?" Lacey asked and leaned her head back and kissed his cheek.

Cole turned her around to face him and opened his hand. Lacey looked down at the heart-shaped gold locket resting on his palm. She picked it up and turned it over. On the back was an inscription that read, *'you hold my heart in the palm of your hand, now and forever, Love Cole'*.

Lacey looked up at him with watery eyes, "It's so beautiful. Thank you."

Cole took the necklace from her and put it around her neck. "I'm glad you like it' he sighed, "I remember how upset you were when you realized you lost your other necklace after your first shifting. I hope this one means as much to you as the other one did."

Lacey rested her hand on the side of his face and stared into his eyes, the amount of love she saw there was breathtaking. She couldn't bring herself to tell him that the necklace he mentioned was actually a choker, and had been a gift from Jesse.

Cole had made remarkable strides over the last couple of weeks in letting go of his past and it was time for her to do the same. She smiled and wrapped her hand around the locket as it rested against her chest. "This means more to me than you can possibly imagine. I'll cherish it forever." She placed a tender kiss on his lips.

Cole grinned. "Ready to go hunting?"

Lacey stepped away from him and glanced toward the woods surrounding their cabin. Her plan had been to tell Cole her news after she proved to him that she was capable of following her natural wolf instincts and bringing down a prey all on her own.

But she just couldn't wait a moment longer. She let out a deep breath to ease her nerves. "I'm pregnant."

"I know" Cole said with a huge smile. "That's why you want to go hunting. Your body is craving fresh meat."

She gave him a confused look. "But how did you know?"

He rubbed his thumb across her cheek lovingly. "A woman's scent changes slightly when she becomes pregnant. It's barely detectable right now, but I'm so attuned to your scent that I noticed the change almost immediately."

Lacey wasn't sure how she felt about hearing that everyone was going to know she was pregnant before she was ready for them to. She pushed the thought away and looked at Cole nervously, "how do you feel about it? I mean, we never discussed when we would have kids." She sighed, "you even told me once that you didn't want children."

Cole pulled her close to his chest and hugged her tight. The conversation that she was talking about played back in his mind. He was a different man then. He had been filled with so much rage and pain. He couldn't believe the things he'd said to her back then. "I'm the happiest man in the world right now" he said and placed his hand over her stomach. "This is my second chance at the life I should have had."

Lacey smiled and threw her arms around his neck. "I love you so much." Tears of joy slipped from her eye as she held onto him as tight as she could.

"I love you too and the little one inside you" he said then paused when an unwanted thought suddenly popped into his head. His body stiffened a second before he forced it to relax. But Lacey still noticed his reaction.

"What is it?" she asked, alarmed.

Cole stared at her, unsure how to respond. He didn't want to upset or scare her, but he couldn't help but think that their happily-ever-after might not be as easy as they wanted it to be. "What about your powers? Do you think the baby might inherit your abilities?"

Lacey's eyes widened. "I haven't even thought about that. What if the baby is born with the same powers I have?" A look of fear crossed her face. Memories of her childhood instantly flashed in her mind. "I was never able to control myself when I was younger. Or what if something happens and I lose control while I'm pregnant? What if the baby gets hurt because of me?"

Cole could see that she was starting to panic. He cradled her face in his hands. "Nothing is going to happen" he said to calm her down. A broad smiled crossed his face, "and if the baby does have your powers then we'll deal with it the best way we can. Besides, having a kid that can move things with his mind will definitely keep us on our toes. It might be fun" he joked.

Lacey rolled her eyes. "Yeah, you say that now. But you might think differently if you get thrown through a wall because your toddler has a temper tantrum."

Cole could sense the sadness swelling up inside her. He knew she was talking about herself and what had happened with her father. And it made him sad to know she was still hurting from his abandonment. "Lacey, you have to know that I will never leave you and our child. No matter what. Even if I get tossed all the way across the mountain, I'm not going anywhere. My home, my life is with you. You're stuck with me until we take our dying breaths."

"Promise?"

"I promise" Cole replied with a kiss to her forehead. "Now how about that hunt? Afterwards, I think you should share our good news with Maggie, before she finds out on her own and comes looking for both of our heads. If she isn't the first to know, she's going to make our lives hell and look perfectly prim while doing so."

They both laughed as they stepped from the porch, shifting into their wolf forms before running off to the first of many amazing adventures to come.

As a thank you to all the readers and fans of The Lacey Hannigan Novels, I've added a free mini novella to the end of the book. It is titled "United" and it's the story of Maggie and Luke's mating ceremony.

Hope you enjoy it!

United

"I can't believe this day is finally here" Maggie gushed as she scurried around her cabin in preparation of the nights big event. "I mean I've known for years that Luke and I would be mated one day but the last few weeks have just gone by so fast."

"You aren't getting cold feet, are you?" A tight voice from across the room asked.

Maggie's head snapped in Mira's direction. She had taken a break from stringing flowers to glare at her.

"Of course not" Maggie said defensively. She glanced around the room at the other six females looking at her. Her eyes met Lacey's. "You know what I meant, don't you?" she asked.

"Yes, I do. And so does Mira. She's just trying to give you a hard time" Lacey said and shot Mira a warning look. "It's natural to be nervous."

They had spent the last three days working on hand-made decorations for Maggie's mating ceremony because it was what she wanted. And to say that they were tired and on edge was an understatement. When Maggie first asked some of the pack females to help with her ceremony, to her surprise, they eagerly accepted the offer but none of them had any idea how much work she wanted them to do.

Maggie flopped down on the couch beside Lacey as Mira and the other women got back to work. "Sometimes, I just can't figure Mira out" she whispered.

Lacey let out a small laugh. "You're not the only one. But hey, just be happy she's not trying to break you and Luke up anymore. She seems to have accepted that you guys belong together."

"I know" Maggie admitted, "that's the weirdest part. Since the whole thing with Jesse, and you getting shot, it's like she's a different person. She doesn't act like she hates me anymore. I mean we're not friends or anything, but we do talk sometimes."

"That's good" Lacey said with a smile. "She is going to be your mother-in-law so to speak."

They both looked across the room. Mira was laying into Kim, a young woman about the same age as Maggie, for not tying the end of the string to hold the flowers in place. Kim looked like she was about to cry, but Mira kept yelling at her.

"Yeah, I'm just thrilled to be related to her. Can't you tell?" Maggie said sarcastically. She blew out a deep breath and looked at Lacey. Her eyes fell to her growing belly. She smiled then shook her head. "You know, ever since Mira heard about your pregnancy, she's been hinting that Luke and I should get started on a family of our own as soon as the mating ceremony is over." She laughed nervously.

Lacey laid her hand over her stomach, a broad smile stretched across her face. Every time someone mentioned her baby, she felt overwhelmed with joy. She was only three months pregnant, but she was already showing. "Well, how do you feel about it? You shouldn't let Mira talk you into something you're not ready for."

"I know. And I won't. But the problem is I don't know what I'm ready for. When I see how happy you and Cole are, I want the same thing you have. I'm just not sure if I want it now or later."

Lacey put her arm around Maggie's shoulder and squeezed her close. "You'll figure it out. And whatever you decide, you know I'll be here for you and so will Kindal."

Maggie's face lit up at the mention of Kindal's name. Over the last few weeks, they had surprisingly become really good friends. Once they realized that Lacey wasn't going to choose between them as to who she liked best, they eventually put aside their jealousy and found that they had a lot in common.

"Where is Kindal? She was supposed to be here first thing this morning with the rest of the girls" Maggie said and stood up. She put her hands on her hips. "If she thinks she's backing out of being in my ceremony, she better think again. She promised to be here."

Lacey couldn't hold in her laughter. She pointed to the dresses hanging up by the front door. "Yeah, she did but that was before she saw what you had in mind for her to wear. Kindal is not a frilly kind of girl. I think the dresses scared her away" she joked.

Maggie's eyes widened. "What?" She walked over and picked up one of the three identical dresses. She held it out in front of her and looked at it. "How could she not like this? It's beautiful. You and Mira haven't said anything about your dresses, so why would Kindal have a problem with them?"

Before Lacey could respond, Mira spoke, "I haven't said anything about them because Luke and Jeremiah warned me I better not. They said I should wear whatever you want me to even if it is the ugliest thing I've ever seen. And Lacey hasn't said anything because she doesn't want to hurt your feelings."

Maggie looked horrified at Mira's response. "Is that true?" she asked and pierced Lacey with a teary-eyed stare.

"No! It's not" Lacey said and went to stand beside her. "I think the dresses are fine. But I also think you're stressing over everything way too much. Just relax." She turned her attention to Mira smirking behind her, "and you should be more supportive."

Mira narrowed her eyes slightly. "I am being supportive. I'm letting the ceremony happen, aren't I?"

Lacey had to bite her tongue to keep from starting an argument. She turned her back to Mira and faced Maggie. "In a few hours you are going to be mated to the love of your life. That's all that matters, right? Don't worry about what Mira or anyone else says about the dresses or anything else."

Maggie looked deep in thought for a minute. "You're right. I'm not going to let anyone get me down today." She put on her usual cheery smile and began barking orders to her helpers about other things that needed to be done for the ceremony.

Lacey and Mira were left standing together by the door. They watched as Maggie fluttered around the room, talking with each of the females.

"Did you have to tell her what we thought about the dresses?" Lacey asked Mira, in barely more than a whisper.

She chuckled and cocked her head to the side. "I agreed to stay out of Maggie and Luke's business, but don't take away all of my fun. Those dresses are hideous and we both know it." She playfully jabbed Lacey with her elbow, "at least I had the guts to tell her the truth."

Lacey tried to hide the smile creeping across her lips. Her new friendship with Mira was surprisingly refreshing and aggravating at the same time. "Whatever. Just be nice."

Mira smiled and raised her brows tauntingly. "I'll try." She opened the door to the cabin and slipped out before Maggie could see her leave. "I'll be back before the ceremony" she whispered to Lacey before easing the door closed.

The next couple of hours ticked by very slowly.

*****

"Are you ready for your whole world to change, Luke?" Cole asked as he buttoned up the black silk shirt he'd just put on. It was the only thing Maggie approved of when she went through his clothes looking for what he should wear.

"He's ready" Jeremiah said from a few feet away. He looked in the mirror that everyone was trying to use at the same time, and brushed his long hair back before putting it into a ponytail at the nape of his neck. "Right, son?"

Luke looked from Jeremiah to Cole as he fumbled with the tie that Maggie had insisted he wear. "Um…yeah, I'm ready."

A loud, rumbling laugh filled Jeremiah's cabin. Everyone turned to look at Scotty sprawled out in a recliner chair across the room. He stood up and started toward them. He stopped beside Luke and hit him on the back. "Man, you look anything but ready for your whole world to change" he teased. "You're shaking like a leaf in a windstorm."

Luke let out a low growl and narrowed his eyes at him. "I'm fine."

"If you say so" Scotty said and walked back to his chair with a big smile on his face. But instead of sitting down, he looked out the window. He saw Kindal and Dean walk by, no doubt on their way to the village for the ceremony considering how they were dressed, and decided to join them. "I'll see you guys in a little bit. I'm going to go and make sure everything is ready."

Nobody said anything as Scotty left. Luke looked at himself in the mirror. Jeans, a dress shirt and a blue tie was what he and Maggie agreed he would wear. It was much better than what she had originally wanted - a three piece suit. Luke was horrified when she told him. Luckily, he was able to get her to compromise.

Cole and Jeremiah passed worried looks to each other. Neither wanted to say it but Scotty was right. Luke was scared. And he was shaking. Jeremiah rested his hand on Luke's shoulder. "Is everything alright? You seem tense."

Luke looked at his dad and let out a deep breath. He flopped down on the sofa behind him and looked at the floor. "I am tense." He looked up at Jeremiah. "What if everything changes between me and Maggie after we're mated?" He sighed, "don't get me wrong, I love her more than anything in the world. She's my best friend. And I want to be with her forever but what if she's not happy with me, the way I perform" he said hesitantly.

It took Jeremiah and Cole a minute to comprehend what he meant. When they finally understood, Cole looked like he suddenly had somewhere else to be. His gaze shifted uncomfortably between Luke and Jeremiah. "I...uh...need to go find Lacey. I'll see you two in a little bit" he said and made his way to the door.

Once they were alone, Jeremiah sat down beside Luke. He could tell his son needed a pep talk. "Luke, it's alright to be nervous and even a little scared. Binding yourself with another person for the rest of your life is a really big deal." Luke looked up at him as he continued to speak, "what you and Maggie have is so special. You knew when you were just a child that she was the one you wanted and she feels the same way about you. Becoming mates is the next step in your lives together."

Luke nodded and looked away. "I know, dad. I'm just worried that I won't make her happy."

"Everything will work out the way it's meant to. You have to remember that this is all new to Maggie too. She's probably just as worried as you are about whether or not she's going to please you. Love is the most important thing in a relationship and you two have a ton of it. Everything else will fall into place."

Hearing his father's comforting words, calmed Luke's nerves. He smiled and gave Jeremiah a hug. "Thanks, dad."

"Glad to help." He looked at Luke with the pride of a father then glanced at his watch. "I should go and find your mom. It's almost time."

"I'll be right behind you" Luke said as his dad left. He just needed a few more minutes to pull himself together.

*****

A knock at the door interrupted the chaos going on inside Maggie's cabin. She rushed to answer it while everyone else was busy getting dressed and doing their hair.

"Cole" she said with a roll of her eyes. "Why am I not surprised to see you here even though I specifically told you that Lacey would meet you in the village?"

He smiled broadly. "You look beautiful, Maggie. But you know as well as I do that I can't stay away from my mate very long."

She pushed the door open all the way before turning and walking off to finish getting ready. Cole stepped inside, his eyes searched the room until he found Lacey. She was sitting on a bar stool in the kitchen with a plate of food in front of her. Two females were sitting beside her, talking but she wasn't listening. She was focused on the meat she was about to eat. Suddenly, she spun around on the stool. Her eyes locked onto Cole.

"What are you doing here?" she said and started toward him. "I was just thinking about you."

They hugged and Cole looked around at all the women hurrying about. Some were looking for their shoes, while others were complaining about missing make-up. Lacey was the only calm woman there. He smiled at her. "Do you have any regrets?" he asked and nodded toward the women yelling and arguing over little things. "About not having a real ceremony when we became mates?"

Lacey shook her head. "Definitely not. We did it our way and this…" she paused and waved her hand around the cabin, "is Maggie's way. I'm happy for her but I prefer the no hassle, less is more kind of things."

Cole kissed her forehead. "How's my boy doing?" he asked and rubbed his hand over her belly.

Lacey raised her brows. "He or she is doing fine" she said and smiled. "Why are you so certain it's a boy anyway?"

"I just am. Six more months and you'll prove me right when the little guy is born."

Lacey looked doubtful. "Where is my bracelet?" Maggie yelled, interrupting any response Lacey may have had to Cole's assumption.

"I think it's time for me to go" he said and nodded toward Maggie, "before she decides to take out some of that pent up tension on me for being here."

Lacey laughed and kissed him quickly then pushed him toward the door. "See you in a few minutes" she promised. She closed the door and was immediately snatched away from it by Kindal. She glared at Lacey with mock horror, "please help me. Tell Maggie not to make me go out in front of everyone wearing this." She pointed to the bright yellow dress riddled with ruffles that she was wearing.

Lacey laughed and shook her head. Then pointed at herself and the same dress that made Kindal look like a fluffy banana. "If I have to wear it so do you."

*****

Jeremiah and Mira stood back by the doctor's cabin and watched as the entire pack showed up and took their seats for Luke and Maggie's mating ceremony. The huge circle of chairs that filled the open space of the village, surrounded a small altar in the middle.

There was some confusion and not everyone knew exactly what was going on since Maggie had insisted on having the ceremony in the village instead of in the clearing where everyone usually had their ceremonies and other parties.

"This is so different from the way things are usually done" Mira said in a low voice so that no one but Jeremiah could hear her.

"I know, but it's what Maggie wants. I think she just wants her ceremony to stand out. To be remembered."

Mira rolled her eyes. "Well, a lot of planning went into this so she better get her ass here soon. Luke is already here and so is Cole" she pointed to the altar where Luke and Cole were standing side by side, talking.

The band started playing. Mira and Jeremiah hurried to their seats and waited for the ceremony to begin. Minutes later Cole was beside them. They all watched as Maggie, Lacey and Kindal came into the village together. Once they reached the circle of chairs and saw Luke waiting, Lacey and Kindal separated from Maggie and went to stand with Cole.

Maggie let out a deep breath as she stared at Luke. Her heart raced in her chest. He looked amazing in every way. For a moment she was stunned to realize that in a few short minutes he was going to be hers forever.

He smiled and she put her hand in his waiting palm. She could feel his body shaking just as much as her own and somehow that made her feel better. He was nervous too. They looked at their circle of family and friends as they slowly walked to the altar together.

Standing in front of the altar was Doctor Sims. He had been conducting the mating ceremonies for over thirty years. He nodded for Maggie and Luke to take their positions on the red silk fabric spread out in front of the altar. They both knelt down to the ground.

Cole and Jeremiah moved to stand beside Luke. And Lacey, Mira and Kindal stood beside Maggie. She looked up at them and smiled. Lacey reached down and rested her hand on her shoulder briefly for encouragement.

Doc Sims called everyone's attention. "On this day we unite this couple with a mating ceremony." He looked at Maggie then at Luke, "Is this what you both want?"

They looked at each other and smiled, then nodded. "Yes" they said in unison.

"Very well. I ask that you turn to face each other."

They did as Doc Sims instructed. Their eyes locked onto each other. The doctor pulled the ceremonial dagger from its sheath on the altar and placed it on the ground between them. "Please repeat these words…

> "Heart to heart,
> Blood to blood,
> I bind myself to you through love.
> In life and death we are one,
> What's done today can't be undone"

Luke was the first to say the vow. He took Maggie's hands in his as he spoke the words that brought tears to her eyes. Maggie followed by repeating the vow back to him.

Luke retrieved the dagger from the ground. His eyes met Maggie's and she saw hesitation in them. She could tell he was worried about hurting her. She smiled to encourage him to continue. He shakily lifted his hand up to her chest. She slid the top of her dress down her shoulders, exposing the upper part of her chest. "Do it" she whispered and closed her eyes.

He looked at her. "I love you" he said a second before he sliced the tip of the dagger into the flesh over her heart. She gasped but quickly composed herself. When she opened her eyes, she saw that he had already cut his hand and was holding the dagger out to her. She looked at it, then at Luke's bare chest. His shirt was open, the tie he had on a moment ago was on the ground beside him.

He nodded at her and she let out a deep breath before leaning over and making a small cut over his heart. Without stopping to think about her next move, she quickly swiped the dagger across her palm. The amount of blood coming from the wound surprised her. She was staring at her hand when Luke took it and placed it over his chest.

Maggie met his eyes and took his hand and placed it over her chest as well. Almost instantly, the stinging and burning from her wounds disappeared as heat flowed throughout her body, warming her from the inside out. Her eyes widened as she looked at Luke with disbelief. His reaction mirrored hers. They stared at each as their blood mixed and a bond formed between them.

The pull they felt toward each other was more powerful than anything either one of them had ever experienced. Desire swelled up inside them. The need to claim each other was instinctual. A deep crimson blush crept across Maggie's cheeks. Luke's breathing became labored as he stared at her. All of the doubt he'd had about not being able to make her happy instantly faded. He suddenly knew without a doubt that he could and would make her happy. He leaned over and claimed her lips in a heat filled passionate kiss.

A loud applause erupted from the pack. Maggie and Luke broke from their kiss looking startled. For a moment they had forgotten they had an audience. They were quickly reminded when several hands were suddenly on them, pulling them up from the ground.

Lacey and Kindal took turns hugging Maggie while Cole, Jeremiah and Scotty shook hands with Luke. The rest of the pack made their way over with their congratulations. But amidst all the well wishes and hugs, Maggie and Luke couldn't keep their eyes off of each other. They smiled and tried to act like they were interested in hearing what everyone had to say but the truth was, they couldn't wait to get away so that they could be alone.

"I'm so happy for you, Maggie" Kindal gushed as Dean held her hand. "It was a beautiful ceremony."

"Yes, it was. Welcome to the family, Maggie" Mira said and surprised her by giving her an awkward hug. It was obvious to everyone there that she wasn't used to hugging.

"Thanks" Maggie said to both Kindal and Mira. They walked off to join the other's by the tables of food set up near the band. Several dozen more people gave their praises before Luke and Maggie were finally left alone with only a handful of people around them. Jeremiah left to join Mira when she yelled for him and Doc Sims soon followed.

Only Cole and Lacey remained. He stood behind her with his arms wrapped around her waist, his palms flat over her belly in a protective manner. He smiled when Luke blew out a deep, exasperated breath. "Bet you're glad that's over with, huh?" Cole said teasingly.

"You have no idea" Luke said. He took Maggie's hand in his, their eyes stared into each other's. It was clear they wanted to be alone.

"Oh, I think we do" Lacey said with a small laugh. She looked over her shoulder at Cole and smiled.

"If you really know how we're feeling right now, then I'm sure you'll understand when I say that we really love both of you but we don't want to be standing here talking to you at the moment" Maggie said in a high strung voice.

Cole threw his head back and laughed out loud as Luke and Maggie ran off, hand in hand toward their new cabin. The sound of his laughter filled the air. Lacey turned around in his arms and kissed his cheek. "How long until you think our little one will have a cousin to play with?" she asked playfully.

He smiled and shook his head as they headed toward the tables with everyone else. He glanced over his shoulder in the direction Maggie and Luke ran. "Not long. Not long at all" he said with another chuckle.

Made in the USA
Lexington, KY
22 December 2014